AN INHERITANCE TO DIE FOR

BONNIE ELIZABETH

My Big Fat Orange Cat Publishing

An Inheritance to Die For
My Big Fat Orange Cat
Mystery 2020

My Big Fat Orange Cat Publishing
MyBigFatOrangeCat.com

ISBN: 978-0-9980829-8-1 trade paperback
978-1-953363-05-3 large print

Chapter 1

Just because I didn't find my cousin Martina dead didn't mean the police, particularly Officer Wilcox, didn't jump to the conclusion I must have done it. After all, Marty, as the family always called her, was mad at me for inheriting Gram's estate leaving her with only a few token items. She'd challenged the will, which was forcing me out of the carriage house where I'd been living in the months since I had learned Gram wasn't doing well.

If that wasn't enough, I was the closest thing to an outsider there was in Seales, Kentucky. I hadn't lived there in nearly fifteen years and I had only come back because of Gram. It might seem strange that a young woman on her own twenty-four hundred miles away would sell her business and drop everything because her grandmother was dying, but Gram and I shared a bond.

Lisa and Barb, two of my friends from acupuncture school, thought I was crazy but they helped me pack up my personal belongings and recommended an attorney to set up a contract so that my associate, Suzanne, could purchase the business in a manner that gave her enough to live on. In all, it had taken me barely a month to get everything sorted and to be on my way in my trusty Honda Fit driving from just outside of Portland, Oregon, to Central Kentucky.

I'd been dating a nice guy named Adam, but it wasn't serious enough that we expected to stay in touch. While we were sad to be parting, he was the one who gave me one final goodbye kiss before I put the car in gear and started my drive. I texted him regularly, but it's not the same as being there, and I knew that soon enough he'd have someone else in his life.

Sitting at the police station in a pale gray-beige room that smelled like a warehouse of cigarettes and stray cat urine, I was rather glad that we weren't together. I didn't have to worry about what he'd think or if he'd believe I had murdered my cousin. Hopefully, he knew better. I had no doubts about any of my other friends back there nor did I have doubts about my immediate family. It was only the other people in

Seales, Kentucky, that concerned me —people who would have known Marty far better than they knew me.

The room I was in was probably ten by ten, not unlike the treatment rooms in my old office. However, the depressing color of the walls and the smell made them far less welcoming. The old table, white laminate with a chipped top, was bolted to the floor. My chair, a metal folding thing that didn't match the two black folding chairs across the table, had a chain around the leg so I couldn't pick it up and toss it. Not that I would, of course.

There was a gray camera in the corner and the glass across from me was no doubt a mirror behind which Officer Wilcox and whoever else was in the department were likely watching me. Now and then the air conditioning turned on with a click and squeak, and warm air was blown about the room. Once I heard people talking in the hall outside but no one came in. No one offered me water.

It's not like Seales has a big department. The town is smaller than some of Portland's better neighborhoods. It was settled by people who were farmers and then by those who had services the farmers needed. Like other areas in Kentucky, they also made bourbon. At some point while I was gone, it had become something of a bedroom community for Lexington but that didn't mean it was much larger. We just got a larger grocery store.

I didn't have much to do while I waited. My phone didn't work well enough in the little interview room which could have doubled as a cell to allow me to do something interesting to pass the time. Even my games were slow. I tried calling my mom but that call didn't go through. I suppose if the police tried to charge me, they had to let me call someone.

Finally, I heard sounds outside the door, the heavy steps of someone walking close by and felt the slight rattle of the table. I heard whispering voices, or maybe they weren't whispering, but it sounded like that through the heavy door.

When Officer Claire Wilcox and another plainclothes officer came in, the door squeaked, a low irritating sound that made the hairs on the back of my neck raise, rather like fingernails on a chalkboard.

Officer Wilcox was slightly younger than I was, tall and willowy with breasts that ought to be implants, not that I've heard they are. It's just that the size of them suggests some sort of augmentation, though it could have been of the lower level kind, such as a well-padded bra. She definitely looks nicer in a uniform than most actresses who play police officers on television and in the movies, which is saying something.

The man with her didn't even seem to notice. He was only slightly taller than Wilcox and his hair was dark to her blonde. His skin was swarthy and the prominent cheekbones made me wonder about Native American heritage of one tribe or another. He was a few years older than Wilcox as well, with lines starting to form at the edges of his eyes. To be fair, they seemed to raise upwards as if he smiled more than he frowned, but maybe I was projecting.

"Ashley Jericho, is that correct?" the man asked, sitting down first.

Wilcox hurried to seat herself beside him.

"That's correct, though I typically go by Ash," I said. I hate the name Ashley. It sounds like a girl who came from money and doesn't have a brain in her head. Maybe that's because I do come from money and I'm cute enough that no one ever thought I had a brain in my head. Besides, I have certain talents that make people think I'm a little naïve.

"Detective Byron Cabot," he said. "You've met Officer Wilcox."

I gave a single tip of my chin. I couldn't say I'd met the officer. She hadn't introduced herself, just come to the carriage house where I'd been loading up the last of my personal items to move to my parents' before the deadline of the lawsuit and insisted I come with her. I'd had to fight to grab my purse and phone.

Fortunately, Gram's houseman, Morgan, had stepped outside of the big house upon seeing the police vehicle and he gave me a nod, letting me know he'd finish getting my personal items out of the carriage house and call my parents.

For all I knew, my mother was trying to persuade my father to get an attorney, right now, just in case. Bad enough that her only daughter had run off to the left coast and studied acupuncture—acupuncture of all things!—and then not returned. She didn't need me coming home only to be arrested for murder.

Don't get me wrong. I like my mother. Mostly we get along just fine. She just never understood why I had to study acupuncture and live so far away when Kentucky was a perfectly lovely place to live. I have to admit that I agreed with her. It's hard to compare the high mountains and stunning views of the Columbia River Gorge with the low rolling greenery of Kentucky, but both have their place and both have their beauty.

It was nice to be so close to Portland while I set up my first acupuncture practice. I had built-in clients because people talked about acupuncture there. I had been thinking I was ready to come home when Gram had taken ill. Gram being ill was the last straw which pushed me to make the move.

"Tell me about your relationship with Martina Beauvoir," Cabot said, interrupting my thoughts.

I drew in a breath and looked down at my hands. I have short, stubby fingers, not at all suited to playing the piano, and my nails were cut unfashionably short. I don't wear polish, unlike many women in the area, nor do I wear any jewelry. Up until a few years ago, I wore a watch but now I use my phone like everyone else.

"Marty was my cousin," I said.

"Marty is Martina?" Cabot clarified. His voice was rough and deep but there was something kind about it, as if he hadn't yet made up his mind.

"Yes," I said. "Marty and I are just a few years apart. As kids we always got along. She was a couple years older than I was, and she often took the lead. We spent a lot of time at Gram's together, though I spent more time with Gram. We kept in touch, mostly by phone and Facebook when I moved west."

Cabot nodded. "Why the lawsuit?"

"Gram left the estate to me, except for specific bequests for Marty, mostly little things. She did get some money out of it, though it wasn't anywhere near what I got. If she hadn't started the lawsuit, I'd have let Marty rent the big house for almost nothing, if that's what she wanted. I like the carriage house out back. It's where I stay when I come back for a visit." I'd gone over some of this for the attorney who was representing me in the lawsuit that Marty had filed to contest the will.

"So you must have been particularly upset about the lawsuit," Cabot said.

"I was hurt by it," I said, already thinking that they wanted me to admit anger. I didn't need an attorney to avoid saying that. "I was also surprised. I never expected that Gram would have left the estate so unevenly to me. I know she wanted me to have the house but not everything."

Though if I were honest, if she hadn't left me everything I couldn't have afforded the house and all that came with it. At one point my grandfather had tried horse breeding. He was too impatient to stick with it, but we still had a small stable which Gram rented out to boarders. Naturally, she hired someone to take care of that so it didn't bring in that much money. So even just the property wouldn't have paid the bills.

Only the bourbon factory did that, and Gram had left all the family shares to me, completely.

"Why did she leave you the house? She knew you lived out of state, didn't she?" Cabot asked.

"Gram and I were close," I said, hoping he wouldn't ask for more. I mean, how was I supposed to say that I was psychic like Gram and could feel the past by touching certain objects? I'd spent much of my time as a child living in her house learning how to block that gift. How was I supposed to tell him that Gram was just as psychic and that I was one of the few who could see the ghost of her beloved Siamese cat, Penelope Blue?

Cabot waited, but I waited him out, just staring at him. I didn't know what else to say, at least not anything else that wasn't likely to get me labeled a loon and perhaps put me that much closer to sitting behind bars.

"Can you tell me where you were early this morning?" Cabot asked.

I wondered if his refusal to give a time were deliberate. "I got up about six or so and started packing. I took a load of my stuff over to my folks, where I'll be living, not long after—the car was already loaded. I was finishing up loading up the last of my stuff when Officer Wilcox brought me in here."

"Did you see your parents?" Cabot was making notes.

"My dad helped me with the boxes. They're mostly books so he used a hand truck to take them inside." I tried to remember what time that was, maybe seven?

"Do you remember what time that was?"

I shook my head. "Maybe seven or so? My mom made breakfast and I ate there before coming back."

Cabot nodded. "Did anyone see you return?"

"Morgan came out to ask if I needed any help with the last of my things and to say he was sorry I had to move out. It's nice for them to have someone in the carriage house. The property is large and having more people around means less chance of someone who isn't supposed to be there hanging out. Gram had a few problems with vandalism and kids loitering. Fortunately her horse boarders are good about knowing who belongs and who doesn't. We're small but Gram hired a groom to take care of the stables and we have someone part time for when the groom is off."

Cabot nodded. "Do you remember what time that was?"

"No, again, I wasn't paying that much attention. Maybe an hour before Officer Wilcox came by? Morgan was just coming out for a break. He normally gets outside about once an hour."

Morgan was paranoid about someone damaging the gardens so he was always looking out when he could. If he went more than an hour looking out or coming out through the door, that was a lot. Of course, seeing a police car, he'd have practically run outside, worried he missed something.

"Then I think we're done here," Cabot said. "We'll probably have more questions as they come up."

He went on to warn me not to leave town, not quite in those words but the gist was clear, however it seemed that assuming my alibi held up, I couldn't have murdered Marty, which was what he was saying.

I'm not sure what's worse. Knowing my cousin was dead or knowing that someone killed her. I didn't even know how she'd died, much less why.

Bad enough that I was a suspect in her murder, at least briefly, though I had no idea if I was completely off the radar, I was vaguely worried that Marty's death might have something to do with Gram's estate. If that were the case, Morgan and Win might be in danger.

And so might I.

Chapter 2

I ended up having to call my dad to take me back to Gram's because while Officer Wilcox had been eager to take me to the station, almost rude, in fact, she was suddenly too busy to drop me at the house, though she'd made like she would in front of Detective Cabot. The dynamic was interesting to me.

I considered asking her why she was so hostile to me in particular, but years of living in the Northwest had made me reticent about asking things that seemed so personal. Also, modern day communications made me wary of her trying to suggest that I was wrong. I've seen too many manipulative patients not to know better.

Seales is the main city in Bram County, squeezed between Woodford County and Franklin

Counties in Central Kentucky. While I might think of it as squeezed, it doesn't mean there aren't distances. Downtown is a fair ways from where my folks live in a little subdivision of large lots and seventies-era ranch homes with basements, some on banks tall enough for the basements to be walkouts, like the house my parents own.

Which meant I had some time to kill on the sidewalk in front of the police station. It's an older building in white stucco and brick. The courthouse was a newer building just behind the station, all fresh new red brick and with a modern sort of federalist look. No domes for us, though. Seales wanted to keep it practical, though there were architects that had submitted proposals for a building with a dome large enough to rival that of any city around.

The cracks in the sidewalk spoke to the age of the place, though everything was clean. Our downtown seemed to alternate between old two- or three-story red brick buildings and those covered half in brick and half in cream or white stucco. The library was an old mansion around the corner. On Main Street, we had the police station across from the city hall, and an assortment of offices and restaurants and even some boutique retail shops like Grace's Chocolates. Grace's was in a smaller house, basically a red brick cottage sandwiched between two large buildings that had always been some sort of commercial buildings.

I always thought that if Seales had had row houses like Boston or New York, the commercial buildings were what the row houses would have looked like. Each of the buildings had two doors, one on either side, with a narrow window without shutters on either side of the door. They rose up three stories tall, all in red brick or red and black brick.

All the buildings downtown were well kept. Four churches anchored the ends of Main Street, two on each end, not quite across from each other, but very close. In the center of downtown was the old movie theater that did special movie runs, usually to raise money for some charity or other. How they stayed in business, I wasn't certain.

A few cars drove past me, certainly not enough to cause any sort of traffic congestion, though I knew making the left turn off of Main onto Park could be a bear. There was always just enough traffic to make you wait, usually until the one traffic signal turned yellow. Then you had to hope no one was going to try and run the light and hit the side of your car.

Geri's Café was making French fries and I could smell them from where I stood. My stomach growled, though I don't particularly like fries, and I'd eaten a good hearty breakfast at my parents'.

Still, when there was nothing else to do, I could think about being hungry.

It was slightly humid but not horrible, for which I was thankful. There wasn't a good place to sit in the police station, unless you were waiting to be processed. I didn't want to stand around in there while the young woman manning the metal detector stared at me, lest I was up to something nefarious.

Finally, my dad arrived while I was pacing around in front of the station. So far I hadn't drawn any unnecessary attention, for which I was grateful. He pulled up in his blue Ford F150. I got in.

"What was that about?" he asked.

"Did Morgan call you?"

"He said you had gone off with the police but didn't know why," my dad responded.

I sighed. I had hoped they'd heard. I was certainly shocked when Officer Wilcox had blurted it out, not even cushioning the news about Marty.

"Did you hear about Marty?" I asked.

"You didn't have to go identify her? I thought that had been done," my dad said. "Her mom called shortly before Morgan did."

"No," I said. "I guess she was killed." I couldn't say murdered no matter how true that might be.

My dad waited, his hands drumming on the

steering wheel as he waited to turn right onto the road out of downtown. It took only a minute but my dad fidgets.

"They wanted to know where I was. One of the police officers thinks I might have done it because of the lawsuit challenging Gram's will."

"What?" my father's voice was low and distracted sounding. Not that I expected he was distracted, it's how he sounds when he's surprised. Like he thinks he must not have been paying attention.

I repeated what I said. I noticed that my father's grip on the wheel got tighter and he started driving a little faster than normal. I was familiar with both those signs of anger from when I'd been a teenager.

Naturally he said nothing further to me. Some fathers yell. Mine gets silent when he's mad. I let him be mad. I was mad myself.

Pretty soon, we arrived at the carriage house.

"Will you need extra time to get your things?" my father asked getting out of the car. "I can call your lawyer and he could get the time extended, I'd think."

"I saw Morgan," I said. "I bet he finished packing for me."

As I slipped out of the car, Morgan came out of the back door of the big house, carrying two glasses filled with sweet tea. Gram had always insisted he have sweet tea on hand or sometimes lemonade. Today was clearly a tea day in his mind.

He stepped off the single concrete step onto the concrete driveway that led around to the carriage house. Several boxwoods and low growing evergreen bushes lined the space between the big house and the drive. As it rounded the back, the narrow foundation plantings grew to a rounded herb garden with plenty of lavender and rosemary. There was even a small white fence that was half falling over under the foliage. It made the place smell good and there were always plenty of bees and hummingbirds around checking out the flowers.

"Miss Ash," Morgan said. "Are you okay?"

"I'm fine," I told him.

Morgan stands just a little taller than I am, his dark, bald head liver-spotted with even darker blotches than his skin. His eyes are nearly the same color brown as his face. He'd been Gram's house man forever. He'd lived in the house, married there, though his wife had passed about a decade ago. He was well paid and smart enough to have done anything he'd wanted, but he'd stayed with Gram, feeling his life of service was the best way for him to be useful.

I know his son sometimes got on him about his profession, but Morgan never complained. These days he was helped around the house by a young woman named Win who bounced and sang and giggled where Morgan stepped with near silence and always with precision.

"Officer Wilcox certainly acted as if she thought you'd done it," Morgan said. "As if."

I smiled a little at him.

My father took the tea and sipped it, thanking Morgan.

"Ridiculous," he finally said.

"Exactly," Morgan said. "But now that bee is gone, she can get to the real work of finding who did do it."

"Why'd she come after Ash?" my dad asked, looking across the yard. It was still green from all the rain, the large laurel bushes and low trees making a private space in the back.

"Didn't you know?" Morgan asked, raising an eyebrow. "Claire Wilcox was one of Martina's best friends, at least lately. The two were as thick as thieves, and if I had to lay money on it, I expect Claire was the reason Marty decided on the lawsuit."

I watched as Penelope Blue faded in on the doorstep behind Morgan. She wasn't quite real looking, just a bit of fuzziness around her that could have been fur. She looked at me with her dark blue eyes and then proceeded to wash a paw. Penelope Blue had a tendency to be around when important things were happening. Whether I was charged or not, this was clearly important.

Not that I really needed Penelope Blue to tell me that this was important. After all, my cousin was dead and I'd been questioned. Things were too far up in the air for me to make sense of everything, particularly as I wondered why Claire would apparently have it in for me.

Chapter 3

Morgan and I finished loading my stuff into the car, and I drove across town to my parents' house. While their home is nice enough, after living in Gram's carriage house for the last few months, my old bedroom was quite a comedown.

My folks had a three-bedroom, two-bath, brick ranch home with a finished walkout basement dating from about the time I was born. They'd rented up in Frankfort before buying the house. My father works in human resources and his company has offices in Frankfort, Lexington, and Louisville. It's a bit of a commute from here, but my mom wanted to be closer to family. My father's family was from Lexington, so Seales was a bit closer to that side of the family, too.

My bedroom was the one in the front corner

of the house, looking over the street. It's a quiet street that ends in a cul-de-sac just a few houses down. Some are ranches and some are two stories, only three of them have basements, which made my parents' house highly desirable. In the summer, most of my friends and I gathered in the basement in the afternoon to hang out because it was cool down there, and my mother didn't bother us very often.

When we were old enough to drive, sometimes we'd head out to Gram's and hang out in the barn or in the big house, someplace Gram wouldn't find us underfoot. Marty was usually with me then, but I hated to think about her.

Inside, my folks' house still smelled of lemon cleansers and pine, cleaning products my mother had used for as long as I could remember. While other people might be changing to more environmentally friendly, Mom stayed old style, mostly. What she has changed doesn't leave off much of a scent and I suspect the smells I associate with the house have seeped into its very bones.

About five years ago, my folks replaced the old, worn carpet and put in a nice walnut finished bamboo hardwood with help from my brother. He's in banking and lives in Charlotte, but when he came to visit on vacation, his girlfriend, who's a real estate agent and fancies herself a house flipper—she's actually pretty handy—helped him and my dad put the new floor in. It looks good, changing the whole look, modernizing the front area, though the kitchen now looks starkly outdated with old pine cabinets and a cream laminate counter.

Mom changed out the old appliances so now they're all stainless, and she'd talked about painting the cabinets, but Abby, my brother's girlfriend, talked her out of it, saying that new cupboards and either granite or quartz would update the value of the place further. To be honest, it didn't take much persuading for my mom to change her mind. It's just a matter of deciding when they want to do it.

If Marty hadn't contested Gram's will, my folks could have stayed at the big house while redoing the kitchen. Mom was set to get a small bequest, a bit more than Marty, about the same as Mom's sister-in-law, Daisy. I got the rest. Oddly neither Mom nor Daisy had a problem with me getting the house.

Marty hadn't even seemed that upset when the will was read. She'd sort of laughed, saying she didn't want the responsibility of everyone looking at her to see what would happen with the big house and the business. I'd probably do a better job.

A few days later she filed the lawsuit. Which

hadn't made sense then and didn't make sense now.

I started pulling in my luggage and the rest of the boxes of personal items I had taken. Someone was mowing the lawn down the road, the faint sounds reaching my ears. The screen door banged on the front of the house as my father headed out to the driveway to help me carry stuff in, having beaten me home by a few minutes.

We worked in silence. My mother wasn't around, having headed off to my aunt Daisy's shortly after she cooked me breakfast. Daisy had called as I was leaving to go collect the last of my stuff, so I'd missed getting the news about Marty from my family and instead heard from Officer Wilcox.

As I brought my luggage into my room, leaving the last of the boxes to my dad, I wondered how Marty had been killed. No one had asked me about weapons of any sort. Had it been made to look like an accident? There were so many questions I didn't have the answers to.

I was just finishing up putting away the clothing in one of my suitcases when my cell phone rang. It was Cheri, one of my best friends from high school and one of the people I stayed in touch with even when I lived on the west coast.

"Hey," I said. I wasn't sure how to answer. Likely Cheri was calling about Marty because we'd all known each other. It's not like Seales was a huge town or anything.

"I'm so sorry to hear about Marty. I can't believe you didn't call me!" Cheri said, sounding almost breathless. I realize that sounds like she's always running, but rather than movement making her breathless, it was often that Cheri talked so quickly about so many things that when she finally paused to take a breath, she *really* needed to take a breath.

"I heard after breakfast," I said. "I was still getting out of the carriage house. If that's changed, no one has told me. Dad talked about calling the attorney."

"That's horrible," Cheri said. "Now Morgan will be there all on his own." Morgan would have been there all on his own with Win no matter what had happened. It wasn't like Marty could just move in. I just couldn't live there.

"Marty dying didn't change that," I said.

"It must be horrible," Cheri said. "Here you were in a fight and she dies and you two couldn't even have made your peace together. You must be ripped up inside."

Actually, I was too much in shock and rather angry with the police and even scared, but I wasn't sure ripped up was the correct word.

"I've been so busy, I haven't even heard how

she died," I said. "I should go over and see Aunt Daisy."

"I'll go with you," Cheri said. "That way if there are any hard feelings, you'll have someone with you."

"My mom is there," I said. "She went over after breakfast, of course."

"Of course she did!" Cheri said quickly. "Anyway, what I heard was that Marty was found in her bed, dead, and it looked like an overdose, although who would believe she actually did drugs, I don't know, which is why the police are looking for who might have murdered her. I mean, they think something like heroin with the needle and all you and know that's not the sort of heavy drug use that she'd do. So you know that she had to be murdered. Did you know her friend Claire was on the police force?"

"I found that out, yeah," I said.

"What do you mean, found that out? Did something happen and you aren't telling me? How can I help if you just let it go and don't tell me?"

"I was taken in for questioning this morning," I said. Cheri might talk a lot and she might like to gossip, but chances were someone else had seen me out on the street in front of the police station and everyone would know by this evening anyway. Even Aunt Daisy, which worried me. Hopefully my mother was talking to her.

"No!" Cheri said. "They couldn't believe that, not even Claire who is not exactly on anyone's nice list but really…it's not like you'd hurt a fly. You help people! You're practically a doctor."

I didn't correct Cheri as she went on about my healthcare credentials. I wasn't practically a doctor. I hadn't studied to be a doctor. I had studied acupuncture, which was a masters level program and had nothing to do with being a doctor. A healthcare provider, yes. Doctor, no.

"I should give that woman a piece of my mind, not that anyone ever really does because she just taps her utility belt, like she's about to draw down on you or something ridiculous and then walks off without saying a word. I swear I got that ticket for not signaling because she knew it was me and she knows I don't like her although I can't say that I'm any different from most of the town. I do not know what Marty saw in her!"

"How long had they been friends?" I asked. "I don't remember a Claire Wilcox when I lived here."

"She moved here about five years ago, I think," Cheri said. "Just from Lexington. I guess she went to the police academy in Lexington but was never hired on over there for some reason so she took the job here. She's never really fit in, although she and Marty hit it off."

Marty worked as a dental hygienist in Versailles. It wasn't a huge commute and she liked the drive. It made me wonder how the two had met. Marty tended to prefer riding horses to socializing, so it wasn't like they met up at something in Lexington.

"How did they get to know each other?"

"I think Claire has a horse out at your Gram's, or she did. I think the place was too expensive for her but she started there when she first moved out from Lexington. She was always complaining about how much she was being charged and how she didn't need all the extras and how she liked caring for her horse. I think I may have mentioned it to you on the phone when it first happened because your Gram was getting tired of hearing about it from Jaci."

Jaci was Gram's head groom—well her only full-time groom. Jaci kept all the accounts, lived above the stable itself, and did most of the work for the horses. We had one other person come in weekly to cover when Jaci wasn't around.

The other barns on the property, from back when my grandfather had done his time attempting to breed racehorses, had long since been torn down or converted to small homes which were rented out. Jaci could have had one, but she said she liked living over the barn. Less of a commute, not that there was much of one.

"That would make sense. Marty keeps her

horse at Gram's and they were probably out there at the same time. What doesn't make sense is that Marty would have let someone go on about the costs," I said.

"You know Marty—she was never one for listening to what she didn't want to hear and likely all she wanted to hear was about Claire's horse. She's a fine saddlebred and I think there were some races involved as well, not that Claire did the riding or anything and I'm not even sure Claire owned the horse at the time. Maybe she purchased it after it retired?" Cheri trailed off in thought.

A racehorse would have intrigued Marty and was probably why they started getting to know each other. Marty would have known about the stables, actually all the stables as she tended to keep up with what was what in the horse world, at least locally. She loved the races and had even gotten Derby tickets a few times. That always surprised me because Derby tickets are not cheap. I often wondered where Marty scrimped, or if those were a gift from Gram.

"True," I said, though Claire's comments niggled at me. Marty might not have been as close to Gram as I was, but I had a hard time picturing her not speaking up if she felt Gram was being unfairly portrayed, particularly by a friend. Not that she'd have said anything, but more likely she'd have just stopped hanging around the person. It made me wonder if Claire had figured that out at some point before she started talking about her problems at the stable. One thing Marty would have understood was finances. If Claire said she found a cheaper place to board her horse, Marty wouldn't have had a second thought.

Cheri chattered on about other gossip and what people were saying. No one had any ideas about who might have done it. Marty had been seeing a guy, but according to Cheri, Landon hadn't been in town.

I didn't push for more information. I mean either he was in town or he wasn't, and it wasn't up to me to find out who did it.

Except that when I hung up and went to check to be sure my father was done with the boxes, I noticed Claire Wilcox sitting in a cop car across the street. She didn't wave when I did. She just sat there and made it very clear she was watching me. My stomach sank as I realized she was going to dog my steps until this murder was solved. If she was busy watching me, who was out looking for Marty's murderer? I could hope Detective Cabot was but I couldn't be certain.

Chapter 4

After sharing glares with Claire Wilcox, I walked back into the house. Through the sliding glass door, I saw my dad out on the deck with his cell phone. He's not much of a talker so I had a feeling he was on the phone with my mom.

I ran my hands over the bannister of the basement stairs as I looked out at him, wondering if I ought to go out and tell him about the police. I moved forward and my hands rubbed the sofa. I wasn't paying attention and I got a moment of intense memory of getting the sofa and how happy my mom had been.

She'd wanted a sectional for the room for a long time. It wasn't a huge room and our old sofa had partially blocked the entry to the living room, bumping up tightly to bannister. You had to step around it carefully because the wall that came out from the dining area meant you couldn't walk easily around the thing. All in all, it made the house, which isn't that small, feel smaller than it should have.

The sectional wrapped around, giving us even more seating area but allowed us to walk through the paths of the rooms as they were meant to be used. It was a blue-gray fabric with no print. It had been brighter then, and I drifted into a trance with the object, watching my fourteen-year-old self jumping over to be the first to sit on it while my mom looked on laughing.

I pulled my hand back not wanting to get further caught up in a twenty-year-old memory. It was easy to do when I read an object, particularly one that brought back my own good memories.

My dad was still on the phone, so I hadn't stood there watching for too long. The ease of watching yourself at a happy time was something Gram warned me about. She'd also warned me about getting pulled into someone else's memories and emotions.

I sighed. I wished I could talk to her about what had happened to Marty. Who would want to kill my cousin? She could be annoying and I was frustrated that she'd contested the will, but she was Marty, my cousin. Family was important.

It hit me then that Marty had touched a

bunch of things, both in her mother's home and at Gram's. There might be a clue in one of her recent memories. I couldn't go to Gram's, at least not unattended by someone like my attorney, probably joined by Marty's attorney. Of course, would there still be a case if Marty was dead?

As it was the weekend, I wasn't going to call and try to find out. That would wait.

I might not be able to go to Gram's, but there was no reason I couldn't go to Aunt Daisy's. She'd expect it, wouldn't she? I went out to the deck to talk to my dad.

The late summer trees were heavily green and the day was already humid enough and warm enough that cicadas were singing. My dad was mostly nodding at the phone and saying umm hum frequently. He glanced up at me and I mouthed the word "mom."

He gave me a nod and continued to nod at the phone, as if my mother could see that he was paying attention to her by the movement of his head through the phone.

"Maybe we should go over there," I said in a low voice, cocking my head to one side.

My dad frowned and continued with his non-verbal side of the conversation. If Mom was upset, she probably wasn't hearing what my dad wasn't saying. I waited, counting my breaths. I got to thirty before I started to fidget. I noticed my dad was tapping his fingers on the table like he taps them on the steering wheel when he's driving. He was getting impatient with my mother.

I said a little louder, "Why don't we go over there and you can talk to Mom at Aunt Daisy's?" I hoped that my mom heard that through the phone and whatever she was telling my dad would pause.

"I can't," my dad said, still talking into the phone.

I wondered what Mom was saying.

"Because I'm talking to you," my dad responded as if that was the most obvious thing. A few more uh huhs and then he rang off, looking at me.

"That was your mother," he said.

"I know," I replied. I tapped on the table as well. It was an older glass model and there were all sorts of water spots, memories of past rainstorms, on the glass, but it had held up nicely. My mom took good care of it. The chairs were about the same era with white metal frames. Mom had just recently replaced the cushions, which she did about every other year. This time she'd gotten turquoise cushions with little white cats on them, probably a hint to my dad that she wanted a cat but hadn't gotten around to talking to him about it.

Normally my mom gets cats when they show

up at the doorstep and she starts feeding them. Pretty soon they're in the house having become ours. She'd been cat-less for almost a year now, the longest I ever remember her without one. She was like Gram that way. Always a pet.

"She said that Daisy has been hearing that you were taken into the police station for questioning," my dad said slowly, trying to find the right words.

It was like being stabbed. My own aunt thought that I would kill her child?

"Daisy is quite upset about it and there are a few women there who are gossiping. Your mom doesn't think it would be good for you to come by just now. She asked that we wait about an hour because by that time the gossips will be gone. Your mom made it sound like you were still moving out of the carriage house to comply with the terms of the lawsuit."

Which gave me an excuse to not be there, other than being arrested because I had killed my own cousin. While I love Seales and I love that it's a small town, sometimes it can get frustrating. This was definitely one of those times.

Chapter 5

An hour later, I was pushing my dad out the door to go see Aunt Daisy. I had gotten a text from Win, Gram's housekeeper, saying she'd heard about what had happened and knew I couldn't do anything like they were saying.

I hated the term she used, as if everyone was talking about me possibly killing my cousin, which I had not done. I understood how people would immediately jump to the conclusion that Marty challenging my inheritance would give me motive to kill her, but that didn't take into account whether I had the ability to do it, nor did it take into account any evidence. But that's a small town for you.

Walking out the front door along the L-shaped concrete path that led to the driveway and my dad's truck, along with my car, I noted that Officer Wilcox was still in her police car. The black stripe down the side with Seales Police in bright white letters made it very apparent that she was there officially. She glared at me as I walked and didn't take her eyes off of me. I hated doing it, but I looked away first and the hairs on the back of my neck were raised as I felt her heavy stare upon me.

"Do you think that could be police harassment?" my dad asked, glancing over at her.

"She's just sitting there. Arguably, if we make a big deal about it, it might keep the department focused on me," I said.

"Did you call your attorney?" my dad asked.

"You mean Nick Spencer?" Nick Spencer was the attorney who was representing me while Marty contested Gram's will. Spencer's firm was the firm who handled wills and other paperwork. I'm not sure he'd know what to do in a criminal case other than tell me not to talk.

My dad nodded.

"He doesn't do criminal law," I said. I hated to call on a Saturday, too. I had learned that he charged more for Saturday hours, unless of course he chose to work them. "I figured that unless I get arrested or I'm held at the station, I'll wait until Monday to call for a referral."

"I just left a message with the answering service," my dad said. "I said it wasn't urgent and that he didn't have to call me today."

Office Wilcox made a point of pulling out and staying on his bumper.

"I think she's tailgating me," Dad said. "Do you think if you called the police they'd send someone out?"

Who knew at this point? "Maybe you should just stop quickly for a small animal darting out into the road and make her rear end you."

My dad chuckled a bit at that and continued driving well below the speed limit to Aunt Daisy's. I hoped that the gossips were gone because having a police car follow you and glare at you the whole time you were with your family was really going to get tongues wagging.

Daisy doesn't live far from us, but the homes where she lives are smaller and the yards were tiny. My mom's brother, my Uncle Ted, had died in a car accident about two years ago. Everyone said it was part of what sent Gram's health into decline. She just couldn't believe she'd outlived one of her children and didn't want to outlive another.

From images in the house, those things I picked up when I wasn't paying attention to not picking things up, I thought they were probably right. The first time I held an old family photo of Gram, Grandpa, Uncle Ted at about eighteen, and my mom just a few years younger, I thought I was going to pass out with grief. My chest got so tight with pain that I couldn't take a deep breath. An ache like an icy pole ran through my entire body and I could hardly stand. My stomach threatened return anything I'd eaten. Before it did so, I'd pulled my hand away, more aware than I wanted to be of the depths of grief that another could go through.

By that time, I'd handled enough things to know that I am generally protected from the emotions that come through the objects I hold and read, whether I'm paying attention or not. The thought that Gram had more pain than I'd felt in that moment just about destroyed me. I could only imagine what Daisy was going through having lost both her husband and her daughter. Even Gram had to admit that she'd had a long, full life before she'd been hit with such grief. Daisy was much younger.

My eyes teared just thinking about it, and I had to wipe at them as we drove up to Daisy's.

Her street was filled with older pin oaks shading the yards. The houses were all built about 1950 or so and ran to three small bedrooms or two larger ones, usually with just one bathroom. Uncle Ted had added the master bathroom and expanded the house out the back, so Daisy's was a bit larger. The trade-off was that they had almost no backyard to speak of.

The one car garage was off to the side. The house was faced with old red brick set with gray mortar. It was the same as most of the homes on the street. A few of the other homes had white-washed their brick, probably after a long bout with HGTV. While washed brick looks nice, if you don't keep it clean in the rain, it shows all the mud and dirt. I knew that because one of the neighbors was less than conscientious about cleaning.

Mom's car was in the single driveway. There were three others parked in front of the house. Abigail Burns, who lived two doors down, was in her yard weeding, keeping an eye on everyone going in and out.

Dad pulled his truck up in front of her yard and I stepped out as he shut off the motor. Abigail would give me a sense of what the neighborhood thought.

"I was worried you wouldn't come," she said, rather kindly. "All that business with the police when everyone who's ever known you knows you aren't the sort to kill someone. But they all think you're not here all the time so you must be guilty. It couldn't be one of them. It's easier to gossip about someone they don't know well."

Abigail was about ten years older than my mom

and her hair was gray but she was still active and spry. She'd never been married to my knowledge and had worked at the library for most of her life. She had a pug that she adored. He wasn't out in the front yard with her, which meant there were probably too many people coming and going for him to remain settled.

"I had to finish clearing out my things," I said. "I didn't know about Marty until this morning. It seemed wrong to go demanding my attorney find out if I still had to move out. Most of my stuff was already at my folks anyway."

Abigail nodded. "There are those who like the gossip, so you be warned, but I know you didn't do it."

Officer Wilcox was slowly cruising the street trying to find a place to park.

Abigail glared at the police car. "What a waste of my tax dollars having you followed."

By that time my dad was out of the truck and waiting on the sidewalk. He greeted Abigail and turned slightly, giving me an excuse to go catch up with him rather than talking to Abigail all morning. The older woman nodded at me and went back to her gardening.

Dad led the way up the two brick steps to the door. The screen door was older and black. There were patches where it looked to have started to rust and that made me sad. Everything was getting older and changing.

My dad knocked on the blue door with its three square windows across the top and then opened it without waiting for someone to come. We normally didn't at Daisy's nor did she or Marty at our house. We only rang the bell at Gram's because she liked Morgan to be sure the door was always solidly closed lest one of her cats get out. Morgan was looking after the two she'd left behind, both chocolate point Siamese like Penelope Blue.

Inside, the small living area was crowded with people. Nancy from church was in the club chair that sat to the side of the sofa. Daisy sat on one end of the gray sofa and my mom was next to her, squashed in by LeAnn, who lived behind Daisy. LeAnn had a son in my class and he'd gone off to Charlotte to manage a bank, as if there weren't enough banks in Seales. Per capita, we probably had as many as Charlotte but we did not house any bank headquarters, forcing him out of town. Of course, I shouldn't be snotty. My brother had done much the same, though he worked for a corporate office of a bank and didn't actually manage a branch.

Apparently, when it comes to LeAnn, I'm a snob.

Pastor Francis, a large man whose head nearly hit the ceiling, was standing by a wall, trying to make himself smaller. He was one of the few

Lutheran pastors in the area. As most people were mostly Baptist or non-denominational Christians, our church was small, and it always struck me as ironic that we had the largest pastor.

"Ash," my mom said, looking a bit horrified as she glanced at LeAnn, who let her eyes fall to the floor.

"Mom," I said, walking over to Aunt Daisy to give her a half hug. She didn't stand for me so I had to bend down and put my arms around her.

The door opened behind me, and I glanced around.

"Mrs. Beauvoir," Claire Wilcox said to my aunt, coming forward, hands out, "I am so sorry about Marty. I want you to know that I'm doing everything I can to bring her murderer to justice."

Daisy stood and glared. "As if you really care. Everything Marty lived for you tried to destroy. I can't help but think that you were behind the stupid lawsuit over the will. While you might argue that you have to be here, I'd like you to leave so I can grieve in peace."

Chapter 6

Whatever I had expected when Officer Wilcox came in, it wasn't that. LeAnn's face turned a bit red as she watched Aunt Daisy give her little speech to the police officer, but she said nothing. Clearly she was one of the gossips Abigail had talked about moments before.

Wilcox stepped back in the small room, practically knocking into me. I wasn't the only one surprised by Daisy's outburst.

"I realize it can be hard when things go bad between family members, but that's no reason to point blame," Wilcox said.

"There's no reason for you to point blame at my niece, either, is there? Sure there's the lawsuit, but as everyone can tell you, Ash was busy moving out of the carriage house at the time my daughter died, so she couldn't have been involved. Further, her attorney warned her against talking to Marty outside of council chambers, something that Marty never expected to happen. She and Ash hadn't even seen each other, something that bothered Marty to no end. Your focus on Ashley is letting the real killer go free, unless, of course, that's your intent." Daisy sank down on the sofa.

I wanted to rush over and go to her, perhaps see if she needed something. It's in my nature to want to help, even if there really isn't any help to give. However, I had learned in acupuncture school, sometimes just being present with another can be very healing.

"I'm sorry you can't see what's clear to me," Wilcox said. "I'll be proving that Marty was killed by her cousin because Ashley's a greedy woman. It's often hard to see our loved ones clearly."

"As I said, there are any number of people who know what Ash was doing during the time my daughter was murdered," Daisy repeated. "You are the one obstructing justice, and I *will* be talking to the chief of police about your harassment. You have no reason to be here. We were not friends and you have been asked to leave. Professionally, you are not welcome here at this time, though I realize there might be questions for me. Accusing my niece of being a murderer with no proof whatsoever in front of her family and my friends is beyond the bounds. Now, please leave before I have to call your boss right this second."

Daisy looked at my mom for help. My mom, bless her, already had her phone and was clearly looking up the non-emergency numbers to the police station.

"If it helps," I said quietly, "I talked to a Detective Cabot. He didn't seem to think that I was anything more than a person of interest."

Wilcox humphed but she was turning to leave. She glared at me as she left but said nothing. I'm sure she was worried that if she gave voice to her thoughts about continuing to watch me, Daisy would have made good on her threat to call the station and try and get through to the chief.

"I'm sorry," Daisy said when the door closed with a click. "You shouldn't have to go through this."

I hurried over to her and hugged her. "I'm sorry, too. You're the one who shouldn't have to go through this." I sniffed, tears that I'd not known I wanted to cry starting to fall.

Daisy and I stood like that for some time, each crying on the other's shoulder. I had no idea how much I needed to know that my aunt believed in me.

"I should be going," LeAnn said, standing up. She gave me a quick, hard glance and then moved to hug Daisy and leave.

My mom patted the sofa where LeAnn had been sitting and I slipped into it, listening to people talk about Marty and trying to comfort Daisy. Pastor Francis came over and whispered with her and then stepped back. He nodded at me and smiled a little. I hoped that meant he didn't think I could kill my cousin either, but who would have thought anyone believed that?

Time wore on sharing memories of Marty. People came and went. My father continued to monitor the door and he opened it and closed it dozens of times. My head started to hurt and I was feeling hungry. People were bringing food. Nancy was up and down putting it in the kitchen.

Several people came in, ate something, had a bit to drink—someone early on had brought those small cans of an assortment of sodas and someone else had brought juice—talked a bit and then left. I got a few funny looks but no one said a word.

When I got up and used the restroom, I spent some time in the hallway looking at photos of happier times.

I reached out to touch a few things but stopped before I did. I didn't want to bring on memories of happier times, times before this where I might get lost. I wandered back to the study, which had once been Marty's room. There were still a couple of stuffed bears, the large-sized plush bears that had been popular for a time. My hand drifted to one of them, knowing even then that these were too old to offer me the sorts of information I needed.

Touching them I was taken back to a time when Marty was crying about not getting the part in a school play. I remembered that. She was in second grade and I was in kindergarten, I think. Half her class was in the play and half got to do scenery. Marty was doing scenery and she had wanted to be on stage.

How often had that happened in her life later on? She'd wanted to be famous and marry well. Instead, she'd stayed in Seales, working as a dental hygienist in a town just as small. She was plenty smart, warm, and funny. She adored her horses and knew people who had racehorses, which was no small investment, yet the young men from those families never seemed to notice her, or if they did, they didn't stick around long.

Even in our family, I was the one Gram left everything to because I had a gift that Marty didn't. She didn't know about my psychic abilities or Gram's. I'd told my mom and that had been a disaster. My mom refused to believe in that "psychic nonsense" as she called it, and I was forbidden from every sharing that information with anyone but Gram. I'd done some sharing when I lived in the northwest, but not much. It's funny how we are often working on being good children long after we've left our parents behind.

I set the bear down feeling sadness for Marty's life, and what she'd done and hadn't done. I wished that she'd had more time to realize her dreams.

As I stepped out into the living area after visiting the study, I thought about all the things I didn't know about her death. It was early in the morning, most likely, and made to look like an overdose. No one believed that, at least as far as I could tell. Maybe it was and Claire was just refusing to believe that Marty did drugs.

I didn't want to believe that either, but I hadn't been around for a long time so I couldn't say for certain that Marty didn't use. I knew that I couldn't have done it because I was clearing out the carriage house. I didn't know when she'd been found and I didn't know who had found her. I also didn't know why she'd been killed. Most importantly, like everyone else, I had not a clue who had killed her.

I was going to have to start asking some hard questions if I were going to clear my name. It was clear that Officer Wilcox was not looking at anyone but me.

Chapter 7

It wasn't long after that my dad and I left. My mom was staying to help clean up. I knew she'd likely be there with Daisy for most of the evening, if not overnight. My mom was close to Daisy for all that they weren't actually sisters but merely sisters-in-law. I tried to remember if they'd always been close, but my mind wasn't focusing on family history just then.

Officer Wilcox wasn't in front of Daisy's when I left with my dad. I wondered if she'd been called to a crime scene somewhere or if she was off duty. I looked at regular cars in case she just wasn't in the black-striped squad car but didn't see her sitting and glaring at me. Nor did my neck prickle with her sharp eyes.

It was getting on towards dinner time and I'd

eaten nothing since breakfast. My dad pulled into the Kroger and we got one of their take-and-bake meat-lovers pizzas. As a healthcare provider, people often think I shouldn't eat stuff like that but that wasn't who I was. I was lucky to have a digestive system that wasn't overly put out by just about anything I ate.

Daisy might have gotten a sample of every type of casserole Seales had to offer, but my dad and I were on our own for food. So, pizza it was.

"Who found her?" Thinking about Marty, I asked my dad the question as we pulled into the driveway. The house looked the same. I had worried just a little that people would decide I'd killed Marty and start spray painting the word "killer" across our garage door, but nothing like that had been done, at least not yet.

"Marty?" my dad asked. He pulled into garage this time. If my mom came home, she'd park in the driveway behind him because I was blocking one of the spots into the garage.

"Yeah," I said, although I wasn't sure who else it would be.

"I'm not sure I heard," he said. "That's odd, though, isn't it? I'd have expected whoever found her to be talking about it."

"Maybe it was Claire Wilcox," I said.

The house still smelled of this morning's eggs and sausage breakfast. My stomach rumbled. My dad went to put the pizza in. I headed off to my room, calling my friend Cheri as I did so. She'd definitely want an update and she might know some things I didn't.

"Did you survive at your aunt's?" she asked.

I gave her a quick summary of what had happened, telling her in more detail than I needed to about Daisy's reaction to Claire Wilcox's appearance.

Cheri cheered on my aunt Daisy about not taking any shit and we both agreed that it was really good of her to do that, particularly now. I added that Daisy's neighbor, LeAnn, was there and seemed to be in the camp that suspected me of killing my cousin.

"Is that LeAnn Vanderplank? She's always been such a gossip. She used to work at the old Seales Marketplace back before Kroger moved into town and I think she got fired because she bad mouthed the manager or something. I guess her husband was really pissed off because it made the next few months in the household really a struggle."

I vaguely remembered that as a sort of scandal, but I think I was already at college, if not in acupuncture school.

"Do you know who found Marty?" I asked, trusting that Cheri, who always seemed to have her pulse on gossip, although she tried to say she abhorred it, would know.

"You know, I was under the impression it was Claire," she said. "Don't quote me because I'm not certain, but it seemed like Claire was the one who found her and then called it in. I could be thinking that because someone else called it in and Claire responded, but it was early for her shift. She doesn't like working the graveyard shift."

I didn't ask how Cheri knew that, but trusted that my friend knew all. You'd think I'd hate to confide in someone so committed to always knowing everything, but Cheri rarely talks about everything she hears. Mostly, she just tells me. Back when I was on the West Coast, I had thought it was because I wasn't in town. I had worried she'd stop when I came back. That hadn't stopped her, and I tried to keep her confidences unless I heard things from somewhere else.

Cheri's secret is that she works as a barista at the local coffee shop. We're too small for a Starbucks, but we have a local coffee place downtown. Most everyone stops in there at one time or another. They also make amazing small batch donuts. They don't serve anything but coffee and donuts, although for kids they have cocoa and for tea drinkers they have tea bags and hot water. They do not serve chai lattes, but I'm probably the only one who might complain.

"So she could have been the one to discover that Marty was dead. Maybe she did it," I suggested, "and that's why she's so eager to pin it on me."

"I doubt it," Cheri said. "Claire is no one's friend, but I don't think she has what it takes to kill someone, you know? Now if Marty killed someone, I'd suspect it was Claire's idea, egging her on and all, but to actually kill someone, I don't think she would."

I always think heart heat when I listen to Cheri. It's a diagnosis that acupuncturists often use when someone talks a lot, almost non-stop. Cheri borders on that. It's only when she gets going that I really think about the diagnosis.

We chatted some more before I rang off so I could go eat pizza with my dad.

"Be careful," Cheri said. "Someone killed Marty and hopefully it will end there, but you read all these mystery books, and well, you know, I'd hate to lose you, too."

Which echoed my thoughts exactly and why I was starting to ask questions about Marty's murder when it appeared that Claire Wilcox wasn't going to be searching for any answers, given that she was already certain that I did it.

Chapter 8

I woke up in the twin-sized bed of my childhood, nearly falling off the side when I did so. Gram had furnished the carriage house with a queen-sized bed in the main bedroom and a single day bed in the secondary bedroom which could be a den or a guest room. I wasn't used to such a narrow mattress. Barely landing on my feet wasn't a good way to start the day. It didn't get any better.

My mom had stayed with Aunt Daisy, and Dad was already up mowing the lawn before it got too hot, or as I liked to say, too light. He usually starts just after the noise ordinance permits mowing. I hoped he'd been careful to do that again today what with Officer Wilcox on my tail.

I glance around my bedroom, which was

painted a sunny yellow. My room was a secondary guest room, though always ready for me, with a more grown up green and gold comforter. My white dresser had been sanded down and refinished to a light maple color. The desk was gone and in its place was a storage bench sitting against one wall. There was a small television on the wall in case a visitor might like to watch TV alone in their room.

It faced the front of the house and I heard the mower going, which might have been what woke me. Looking at my phone, it wasn't as early as I thought, so my dad was, indeed, being a bit more careful.

I dressed quickly and went out to the kitchen. My mom might have welcomed me with breakfast when I moved in, but after the tragedy, I was on my own. I found yogurt to which I added some pecans that I found in Mom's baking supplies. She'd likely get mad at me later on because there wouldn't be quite as many as she needed for whatever she baked, but maybe I'd replace the little bag of chopped nuts for her later on. It wasn't like I had a ton of stuff on my schedule.

I was supposed to be going through Gram's stuff in the big house and figuring out what I wanted to keep and what I didn't want to keep. I had planned on talking to Aunt Daisy about whether she wanted to live in the big house—I was pretty sure my parents didn't, but since the challenge to the will, I couldn't do those things.

That had left me working on getting my ducks in a row for setting up my acupuncture business. I had applied for my acupuncture license in Kentucky and now it was just a waiting game. I had scoped out a few places here that I'd be looking into but didn't want to jump the gun and look too eager. There was also a chiropractor in Versailles looking to hire an acupuncturist and I thought that if the opportunity was still open, I'd talk to her about how she envisioned the set up.

However, I didn't quite have my license and looking at properties felt like jinxing my chances. This felt particularly true after this latest disaster.

I ate my yogurt, watching my father walk back and forth across the lawn pushing the mower, making nice neat lines in the grass. One week he angled them with the upper angle on the left and the next week he'd angle them in the other direction. He liked that.

Personally, mowing lines had never fascinated me. His movement kept me from having to think too closely about anything as I ate and waited for some coffee to brew. I don't always drink coffee. In fact, I usually try to get tea instead as green tea is supposed to have some health benefits, but this morning was definitely a coffee kind of a morning. If I'd been a little more prepared for being questioned in a murder, I would have had some yesterday, too.

I glanced out the front window and saw Claire Wilcox sitting in a dark gray Hyundai Elantra, her blonde hair just visible in the side window. Her hair looked mussed from the angle I saw her. I decided she'd probably slept in the car. If she was being that obsessive, the least I could do was bring her a cup of coffee.

I also thought about what my dad would say about killing people with kindness. If I was just nice enough to her, maybe she'd let go of the idea that I had done it. As I poured the coffee into a disposable cup I found in the cupboard, mentally arguing with myself about whether I should use that or a regular mug, deciding on the disposable in case she threw the coffee at me, I geared myself to hear more about how she knew I was a killer.

I left my half-eaten yogurt on the counter along with my own coffee. I'd be back in a second or two, maybe a minute.

Taking a few deep breaths, letting the smell of coffee fortify me before exiting the house, I walked out the door. Her Elantra was right in front of the house. The car was older but clean.

I started to get a funny feeling as I walked across the grass. Claire didn't move, but she seemed to be looking my way. Maybe she was asleep and her head was turned awkwardly. The turmoil in my belly told me that something else was wrong.

I tapped on the window, hoping that she would turn and sit up and make it all better, but tapping did nothing.

My hands shook, spilling coffee on the ground.

I tried the door handle. To my surprise it opened. Claire fell out of the car, her eyes half opened, her body rigid as it hit the ground.

Her head made an odd smooshing sound when it hit. I thought I was going to be sick as I backed up towards the house, tripping over my own feet as I started to moan and screech in an odd combination of sounds.

I am normally not squeamish, but finding a dead body when you don't expect to can freak just about anyone out. I was definitely no exception, particularly when my compulsively thinking mind started warning me that I had a very good reason to want Claire Wilcox dead.

Chapter 9

John Gardener, the neighbor across the street, ended up calling 911. He'd been drinking his own coffee standing in his front window and saw me backing away and falling down. He'd come running out in sweats and a plain white t-shirt and practically banged into the car. He'd been dialing the police even as he did so.

John was younger than my folks and his youngest son, Troy, had just gone off to the University of Kentucky. His oldest son, Tyler, had gone two years earlier and their house had practically become a UK support store. Their formerly cream-colored door was now Wildcat blue and so were the shutters. They'd been one of the families to whitewash the brick on their house so the blue stood out nicely. Both cars had UK stickers on them, one on the bumper and one in the window.

While I liked John, I was glad he was dressed as well as he was and not just in his underwear or something. I was touched when he confessed he'd originally been worried that Claire had attacked me, and I needed help. I was glad that wasn't what happened as John isn't exactly a physically fit guy. He's one of those people who stays thin no matter what, but that didn't lend itself to muscle or to any particular coordination.

In fact, I'd been asked when I'd visited a few years ago about using acupuncture for a damaged knee from a fall. Then I'd been asked about it for a shoulder injury, also from a fall. If I hadn't seen him fall in his driveway on several occasions, I'd have been worried about spousal abuse, no matter that he was a man.

He'd slid to my side, falling on his back even as the 911 operator answered his call. He'd started speaking nearly unintelligibly until the operator, used to calming people down, asked him to take a few deep breaths. He did, combing his free hand through his thinning whitish hair and was then able to tell her what had happened.

He'd barely finished when I heard a siren, getting louder by the moment. Like police everywhere, those in Seales weren't about to let a murder of their own go free.

My dad had stopped mowing and came around the house to find John and I sitting on the front lawn and Claire's body hanging out of the car. I think he'd have fallen, too, if he hadn't been hanging onto the mower. It's one thing to see someone dead. It's another to see a body hanging out of a car with their head on the edge of the curb.

"Did she fall out?" my dad asked, walking over to us. "Did she hit her head? Have you called an ambulance?"

"John called 911," I said. I didn't tell him that I thought she was dead when her body slid out of the car. From the angle of how she landed I didn't think anyone would get the idea that she'd been alive when she fallen out. I looked away.

The police drove up quickly and a young male officer immediately went to Wilcox and started searching for a pulse. I had no doubt he wouldn't find one.

"What happened?" the officer asked coming over to us after he'd called in something on his radio. I don't do police speak.

John started talking, too quickly, again, and the office held up a hand to slow him down.

I spoke up then saying I'd been the one to find her. I explained seeing her and deciding to be nice and take her a coffee as I assumed she'd been sitting in front of the house since her shift had ended. When she hadn't responded, I'd opened the door in case she needed assistance. Then she'd slid out and hit her head on the curb.

The officer took notes.

Then he took John's statement which included the fact that he was worried Wilcox was attacking me and he wanted to save my life.

This meant that everyone had to explain why Claire Wilcox might be threatening my life which brought up the whole case about my cousin Marty.

By the time everyone was done defending me, I was ready to call my attorney for a good criminal defense attorney because even I believed I had killed Wilcox. While I appreciated the support, their denials seemed a little too forced, if you know what I mean.

I waited, sitting on the ground, wishing I'd never considered taking a cup of coffee out to Wilcox, or at least waiting until I'd finished mine. John got up and dusted himself off. A group of people from the neighborhood were now out in their yards looking at our house. My dad stayed with me, though he'd pushed the lawn mower into the garage. He was sitting on the single step up to the front porch and watching.

Maybe he'd tried to get me to sit with him—I had some vague recollection of that—but I was still sitting on the grass where I'd landed, afraid that if I moved too much some other disaster would happen.

My fingers scraped the dirt, noticing the length of the grass, realizing my dad had started mowing in the back. If he hadn't, perhaps he'd have been the one to find Wilcox. I sort of wished he had.

I pulled a piece of grass, holding it, looking at the green. I let my mind open up but there were no emotions attached to the grass. It was a game I'd played as a child with Gram, always wondering if insects or animals left emotional imprints. Penelope Blue had left them around Gram's house, and I'd found several in her favorite spots. Fortunately, they were all good memories.

I pulled a long, pale grayish-colored weed, probably long dead. As soon as my fingers touched it, I knew it wasn't a weed. It was a wire from a necklace, one of those that had been popular when I was in junior high, a heavier wire that hung around the neck with a single charm on it in the center. This wasn't as thick as that but I knew it'd been used for that purpose because I saw it—mentally, my psychic powers opening up because I hadn't been paying attention and purposely guarding myself.

I saw a young woman excited about a charm from a boy and putting it on the wire. Joy. Excitement. Hopes being dashed. Anger.

I practically threw the item away at the anger. I stopped myself just before letting go. This was probably a clue and I needed to get all the information I could get. I felt layers of anger, old anger, a teenager's anger at being dumped. There was hurt, deep painful hurt that I felt in my heart. But there was also a blanket of current anger around the item, drawing me into it.

Someone was pulling on the wire, not the owner, but someone else, preventing the owner from doing what she needed to do, believed she needed to do. Such anger that she couldn't do her job, that no one believed her. I felt a certainty of being right. A one-pointed anger and a desire to do a job, but someone was stopping them.

Fear reached in at the last moment as the owner wasn't able to breathe and was being dragged backwards. Someone else was grabbing the entire wire necklace, pushing it aside, letting it fall to the ground.

Then nothing. I dropped the wire quickly.

I was almost certain the necklace had been Claire's. Now my prints were on it. As if things couldn't have gotten any worse. I wanted to cry.

Chapter 10

Just as I was coming out of my psychic trance, Detective Cabot arrived. He took in the scene, talked to the responding officer, Officer Myers, and then came over to where I sat. He didn't sit on the grass. Instead, he squatted down easily. Up close, Cabot was clearly a few years older than I was, his skin slightly dry from the sun. There were slight variations of color under his neck, as if he worked outside and the sun didn't quite reach beneath his chin.

This close, he smelled of rosemary and lavender, probably from a shampoo or aftershave. He looked at me with his dark eyes and took in everything. I pulled up the necklace I was holding on the grass before he noticed it on his own.

"I just found this," I said. "I was digging around, didn't realize…"

"It's not yours?" Cabot asked quietly.

I shook my head.

He nodded and called Myers over. "Evidence bag."

Officer Myers hurried over. Other cars were arriving. An ambulance had been there for some time and it was finally leaving, the medics apparently convinced Wilcox wasn't coming back from the dead to need their help.

"We'll need your prints to exclude you," he said.

I was starting to like this guy. I am not the sort of woman who would normally fall for a police officer. I'm way too suspicious of anyone with that much authority. I stay up on all the concerns in the news. I also try to stay out of the way of the police, except, of course, now I was surrounded by dead bodies and I was going to need their help.

"Okay," I said.

Cabot helped me to my feet, his hands warm and dry against my skin, lingering a bit longer than I thought necessary, but when he stepped back, a concerned frown on his face, I figured he was just worried about me being able to stand. Ah, well. He was just doing his job, and I was appreciating the fact that he wasn't arresting me right away. A relationship needs something more to start, doesn't it?

"Tell me what happened." The open-ended question gave me time to tell him about my morning. I wondered how many more times I'd have to tell what had happened. If Wilcox had found Marty's body, then how many times had she had to go over what had happened? Did they believe police more than lay people?

Cabot questioned me nicely. Clearly I wasn't a suspect, at least not at the moment. Either that, or he figured he'd catch more flies with honey, at least to start out. John was questioned next. Now that I was standing, I walked back over to sit with my dad. He patted my knee when I sank down.

"Just not having a good week, are we?" he said quietly, a dry understatement.

Noting his cell phone I said, "Did you call Mom?"

He nodded. "I told her it was under control here. She's pretty upset and worried that you could be next."

I shivered. I had been more worried about being arrested than getting killed but now I had a new worry. I hoped that Cabot was efficient at following the evidence so that I didn't end up as one of the bodies that seemed to be piling up. I didn't remember the last time Seales had had a murder.

I glanced up and Cheri was pushing her way

through the neighbors lining the edges of the property. An officer tried to stop her but she pointed at me. I started to get up, but Cheri was being pushed back into the crowd. I watched as her light brown, nearly blonde hair was pushed further away. Cheri is short so she disappeared quickly behind the taller people in the crowd.

I went inside and grabbed my phone so that I could at least text her that I was okay. I had a feeling I wasn't going to be let out of the crime scene any more than Cheri was going to be let in.

The house was cool after the humidity of the morning. I hadn't even realized the air felt close, I'd been so focused on everything else. Grabbing my phone, my eyes landed on my barely touched coffee and I walked over to it. Cold. And stale. My yogurt was warm. Neither seemed like something I wanted.

I sighed and poured the coffee into the sink. Then I walked back to the porch to sit with my dad. People were talking and they were looking, some at us. I wondered how many more now thought I was a murderer. Maybe they were more worried about the actual murderer starting to prowl their neighborhood. Either way, chances were I wouldn't be welcome.

I itched to go and touch things, things that belonged to Marty. I knew that Wilcox had been strangled, or at least partially strangled thanks to her necklace. Unfortunately, when it was being touched, she hadn't seen anyone. She was in our front yard when it happened, if the placement of the necklace was any indication. It seemed like she was trying to do something.

Was she going to set the house on fire? Plant a camera?

I bit my lip and glanced around. My room was at the front. I stood up and started looking around in the bushes. Officer Myer came over and asked me to sit down.

"I found that necklace in the yard," I said to my dad. "What do you think she was doing there? Was she trying to look through the windows?"

My dad just shook his head, not willing to offer an answer. Gram would have been better. I could have talked to her about the anger I felt and the impressions I had gotten. Clearly the necklace had been important to Wilcox for a long time. I realized then that I had only seen the wire, not the charm.

I considered walking back out to the yard but knew I'd be asked to sit down while the crime scene investigators went about their work. My neck started to ache from the tension of sitting and waiting.

Cabot came up to where I sat. "I can take you to the station to get your prints. In the back of my unmarked car. I'd offer to let you drive yourself but there's no way we'll be clearing a path for you and it would be just as obvious where you're going."

He seemed to be trying to mitigate the stigma of me going back to the station.

"Okay," I said, looking back at my dad.

He nodded. "I'll be here. You have your phone."

I showed him.

Cabot suggested I get a purse or something in case I needed it. He was kind to me, not acting at all like I was a suspect.

I hurried inside and found my things. I looked longingly at the coffee maker, thinking of the cup I hadn't gotten to drink. I wondered if anyone had picked up the cup I'd taken to Wilcox. At this point, I was thinking I'd even like to drink that.

Chapter 11

I got my fingerprints taken. I waited to have an official statement taken—after all, I was already down there. If Cabot believed I was a killer, he was certainly polite about it. It made me wonder why he was being so nice. Unfortunately, although I did try and touch his coffee mug, there were only faint irritable impressions of an average day in a police officer's life, which told me nothing.

When I was done, I called Cheri and asked her to pick me up.

"Are you okay? They weren't arresting you or anything? I heard that Claire was found dead in her car and that she was strangled. No one thinks you have the body strength to do that because I guess Claire worked out with more than just her horse," Cheri said.

"I found something in the grass and they said they needed my prints for elimination," I told her. Hopefully they weren't lying to me about why they wanted them.

I knew I hadn't done anything and this seemed like the best way to eliminate myself as a suspect. I had no idea what an attorney would have said, but I could call Mr. Spencer for a referral tomorrow. Even if they weren't treating me like a suspect now, I wanted to know I could count on someone to help if that changed in the next few days.

"I'll be right there," Cheri said. "I'm parked way down on your street and although they look like they're starting to close down the scene, I'm not sure how long it will be before your dad can easily get out of the driveway. It looks like a block party down there, except, you know, instead of streamers and balloons, there's crime scene tape."

I didn't really smile at the image. Instead I tried to put on a good face as I was once again standing on the street outside the police station.

"I'm going to walk up to the library," I said. "That way if someone hasn't heard about the murder, it doesn't look like I'm a suspect, again," I said.

"No worries," Cheri said. "I'll be there in a jiff."

With that she rang off and I walked up the street to the library. It was well past lunch and my stomach was protesting even though I wasn't sure I could eat. It was hot now, too, and the concrete walk and the blacktop of the road seemed to increase the heat.

I smiled at Tara Morrow, one of Gram's horse boarders, as I walked up the road. She was a tall, muscular woman who had no shape other than the muscular curves on her body. Her dark hair was worn slickly short and she had on large sunglasses, so I wasn't even sure she recognized me until she spoke.

"I'm so sorry to hear about Martina," she said. From the use of her full name, it was clear that Tara didn't know Marty well.

"Thank you," I said. We both paused, awkward in what to say next.

"I hope they find who did it," Tara said. A faint blush crept up her face as she thought about what she might be suggesting. She quickly turned and said she had to go.

It would have been funny if it wasn't about the death of my cousin and the police officer investigating it. Given that Wilcox had still been outside my house, and, so far as I knew, she hadn't investigated anyone but me, it couldn't have been the cliché reason that she had gotten too close to the criminal.

I leaned back against one of the large pillars that sat to either side of the library's door. It was a three-story building, though only two held books. The building was an old Southern mansion with bright red bricks and gray columns. There was one pillar on each end of the front of the building and one on either side of the door. Six tall windows lined the front on either side of the door on each floor, though those on the third floor weren't as tall as those on the first two floors.

There weren't many people out and about on a Sunday morning. Those that got up early were either in church or working their horses. Seales is a very horsey community even if I'm not terribly horsey myself. I ride but that's about it. It's not that I don't like horses, I'm just not horse crazy. I have no idea how that passed me by but somehow it did. Maybe I was too worried about what I might learn if I inadvertently touched the wrong saddle.

I had done that once and it wasn't something I wanted to remember.

I noticed someone walking quickly towards me, fast enough that I barely had time to recognize him before he spoke. My stomach sank. Rick Darlington was not someone I wanted to talk to.

"Ash!" Rick said practically running up me in greeting. His hair had darkened from a sexy blonde to a mousy brown with a few stray highlights that could have been early gray. He'd put on weight, too, but Cheri had mentioned that in our talks. I was surprised that he hadn't found more excuses to drop by the house since I'd been in town.

He'd come to the carriage house once when I first came back and then he'd talked to me at Gram's funeral. This was the first time I'd seen him since. I steeled myself against having to talk to him. My breakup with Rick when I left to go to acupuncture school had been as messy as my breakup with Adam had been easy.

"Rick," I said cautiously, wondering what tack he'd take now. He hadn't been rude to me any of the times I'd seen him but he'd said enough snarky things on Facebook and Twitter that I was always a little worried that some sharp insulting comment was going to come out of his mouth.

"I'm sorry to hear about Marty," he said.

"Thanks." I continued to lean back as he stood looking around wondering what to do. I didn't help him.

"How are things?" he asked.

"We're getting through." I had no desire to share the secrets of being implicated in not one but two deaths. How did he think I was doing?

But given the awkwardness of the situation, I cut him a break.

"Good." He looked at the ground. In high school and through college, Rick had always been confident. If that had changed, no doubt it had to do with the fact that he'd flunked out of UK. Too much partying and not enough studying. He'd said that even when it happened, as if that was going to straighten him up. It didn't. The fact that I was less interested in partying had been one reason he resented me going off to school for acupuncture.

He'd told me he now worked at Larry's gas station, one of the few independent stations left around. It was in a good spot, on the highway to Frankfort and at a traffic signal. Larry's family'd been lucky as times had changed and it was easy for people driving through to stop and fill up.

I watched for Cheri's little gray Ford Focus but I didn't see her yet. If she was parked down the street, she might have had a walk to get there.

"Guess you're probably busy. Will you be out at your aunt's later on?" he asked.

"Maybe," I said. "I was there most of yesterday, though."

Rick nodded and sighed like he wanted to say something else. "Guess it's hard with that police woman after you."

I just nodded as if I didn't know anything. Rick looked disappointed. It was a bit surprising that he hadn't already heard about Claire, but perhaps he was just out of the loop. If he did know anything, he knew she died outside my house, so perhaps he wanted to hear what I had to say. Most gossips would also know that I was the one to find her, although to give him credit, Rick didn't gossip much.

In fact, I couldn't remember anything that he did much of. He liked playing video games, watching sports, and sometimes doing a bit of duck hunting, but he wasn't a big fan of that. He preferred the outdoors to be a little less rugged and rough.

"I guess I'll see you, then," Rick said, wandering off.

I waved at him and heaved a sigh of relief only to have my insides sink as Aunt Daisy's neighbor, LeAnn, came hurrying down the walk.

She looked at me and nodded before entering the library. She didn't blush but she didn't appear ready to hang out with me for any amount of time either. No matter. At least she wasn't the sort to stand around accusing me of murder in front of everyone.

Fortunately, Cheri drove up and picked me up before anyone else came around to perhaps do what I had feared LeAnn would do, point a finger at me and say I had done it. I'd be so glad when the killer was caught. But who was it? Who would do that to those two women?

Chapter 12

I really wanted to go by Gram's but I wasn't allowed in without Marty's attorney which wasn't likely to happen until after an inquest. Still, I wanted to touch things Marty had touched recently. I didn't have a key to get in and check Marty's apartment. If Mom hadn't hated my talent so much, perhaps I could have talked to Aunt Daisy about going over there.

Unfortunately, my mom had felt so negatively about the idea of psychic powers that I hadn't ever dared tell anyone, not even Cheri. It was certainly possible that as a child I had said something, but that was so long ago that we'd both forgotten. I certainly wasn't bringing it back up.

So, because I couldn't go to Gram's, Cheri drove me home, where we got as close as we could. The police were still there but not in the force they had been. Now it was a crowd of neighbors, and my dad was standing in the middle talking to everyone. The voices and discussion stopped when I got out of the car a few houses down.

I paused as heads turned. Clearly the murder was being discussed, along with me. I wondered if my dad was having to defend me, but John was looking, too. I had no doubt he was also defending me unless he'd changed his mind from earlier. As I got closer, passing under the tall mature pin oaks, I smelled freshly mown grass. My dad hadn't been the only one out this morning, though I couldn't remember hearing another mower.

My dad said something I couldn't quite hear as I got closer, and the neighbors turned back to him and started talking again.

Cheri caught up to me. "Well, that's some welcome, isn't it? You don't suppose they've all decided you're strong enough to strangle someone or maybe you're not emotionally strong enough to hear their thoughts on the woman you found dead?"

"Don't you think they'd be running away if they believed that?"

Cheri laughed and wrapped her arm around mine like we used to walk when we were kids, laughing about something that might actually have been funny. This was definitely not.

As I got closer, I saw feet shifting. John Gardener looked at me and smiled. "You're back."

"They only wanted my prints for elimination purposes. I found something on the lawn and I opened the car door," I said.

John nodded. "They asked me to come down to the station tomorrow morning for an official statement. I think they were worried about how much they had to do. I don't think Officer Wilcox was much liked around here. But she was one of their own, so they'll make sure to find who killed her."

"I know," I said. "I hate that she died in front of our house. I know she was Marty's friend. Do you suppose they both knew something?"

Maybe I shouldn't have said that aloud. The thought just occurred to me and I spit it out without really processing it. I'd been focused on the fact that I was connected to both women in negative ways, but what if Marty and Wilcox had been some place and seen something or heard something they shouldn't have? I'd really have to get Aunt Daisy to let me into Marty's apartment for that.

My dad patted my shoulder, "You don't have to worry about that. The police will take care of it."

There were nods around from the neighbors, even those I didn't know. There was one young couple that I'd seen on the street but who hadn't lived there very long. No doubt over time I'd get to know them.

I smiled and slipped out of the crowd with Cheri. Given that there were people who didn't know me the way John Gardener and some of the others did, what would this do to my business? I had hoped that being a community daughter I'd get people into my acupuncture clinic based on my name. Now, though, it was looking like my name was going to be mud. I hadn't even opened the place yet.

"What is it?" Cheri asked as I opened the front door to go inside.

"I was just thinking that I'm going to have to work even harder to build my acupuncture practice after this. Who would want to go to an accused murderer? I know that's horribly selfish of me to think that but…"

I felt like crying again. All the tears I hadn't shed over Marty because I was too busy were coming out now. All the fears, too, were finally hitting me, reminding me that I had probably been in shock all day yesterday. At least I was indoors, away from the crowd.

"Don't worry about that today. Do what you can for now. I bet by the time your license comes through and you find a place to practice, they'll have found the real killer and something else will have happened. People forget, you know, especially today with social media and stuff and the fast news cycle. Why, I read an article about that just last week or something about how we're exposed to so much information that we can't take it all in." Cheri paused to catch a breath.

"I'm less worried about people who know me and more about the people who don't. Like the young couple out there with all the other neighbors. I don't even know their names. They know my name and my face and I have to wonder what they think about everything. How can they know I didn't kill Marty and Officer Wilcox?"

Cheri shrugged. "When the police arrest someone else they'll know. And if they forget because they only remember your name connected to the murders, don't you think that everyone who does know you will remind them that someone else killed your cousin and her friend?"

"And if they don't find who did it?" I asked.

"We won't even go there," Cheri said, looking around the room, deciding where to lead me.

My stomach growled a little.

"When was the last time you've eaten?" Cheri asked, ever practical. Upon finding out I hadn't eaten that day, she set about looking through the refrigerator and checking for food that she could make for me. I let her do that while I called my mom to check in on Aunt Daisy, which I hadn't had a chance to do yet.

Things were about the same and there were still people visiting. They all wanted information about the officer who was killed in our yard. It wasn't exactly correct, but I didn't correct my mom about it. Once again I was the subject of heavy gossip.

On television something would have happened to break the case. Instead, I was in my kitchen, watching a friend make me a sandwich of leftover chicken and feeling as if I hadn't learned anything in the last twenty-four hours.

Chapter 13

I have never been so happy for Monday. I'm not someone who hates my job, so the new work-week has never been an issue. Still, I wasn't usually excited about the day the way I was that Monday. Monday meant I could call my attorney during regular business hours and set up a time to visit the house. I could ask all my questions about what would happen with the challenge to the will, too. Not to mention I could get a referral for a good criminal attorney in case I needed one.

Marty's attorney was from a Lexington firm. Mine was from Frankfort, so I wouldn't be surprised to learn that neither of them knew of her death, unless my dad had mentioned it to Mr. Spencer in his message. I supposed the police might have contacted her attorney to find out what they could about the lawsuit. I had read in some mystery or other that privilege continued after death, but maybe that was only true in fiction. I wasn't a lawyer.

I dressed in jeans and a loose blouse in pinks and blues and greens all splotched together like someone had finger painted on the material. It was one of my favorites and I hoped that wearing it would make me feel better.

I hadn't unpacked much, but I was hoping I'd get news that meant I could move back into the carriage house. While I hadn't nearly fallen off my bed this morning, I'd slept with a leg hanging off most of the night. I was definitely used to a bigger bed.

I also hated that I worried about waking my parents. My mom had come home last night and I knew she was getting some much needed sleep. She'd been up most of the previous night with Aunt Daisy. I couldn't image either of them had slept much. I was surprised I could sleep as much as I did, but it could have exhaustion and my mind's way of saying nope, not the time to deal with this.

I made coffee, eagerly awaiting a cup to wake me up. I needed it today more than I needed it yesterday. I vowed I wasn't even going to look out the window until I had had it. And I was eating breakfast. Having a sandwich in the middle of the afternoon as my only food was not good for me.

I considered making eggs, but I worried that the sound of pans clattering would wake my mom. Instead I had a yogurt, like I'd been eating yesterday. I wondered what had happened to it. This morning I'd heard my father leaving, the garage door going up. He'd probably go in today and then figure out when we needed him most before he took any time off of work. As a human resources manager, at least he knew his work rights.

The yogurt was tasteless but I wasn't sure eggs would have been any better. At least I had something. I cleaned up the kitchen, though there was little to do, and started the dishwasher. I knew from experience that the dishwasher was quiet enough not to wake my mom if she was still sleeping.

By the time I'd finished doing my mini-cleaning, it was late enough to call my attorney. I guess that was one good thing about laying around in a too-narrow bed deciding whether it was time to get up or not.

Nick Spencer worked in the office of Erickson, Carter, and Moss. Gram had worked directly with Mr. Erickson, but he wasn't taking new clients. So when it turned out I needed someone to represent my side of the challenge to the will, I'd been assigned to Mr. Spencer. Mr. Erickson had told me he would be monitoring the suit, but didn't feel that Marty had any good legal challenge to the wording. She'd been remembered by Gram, and it was clear that Gram had been of sound mind and body, having made the will over twenty-five years before, updating details and refiling about every six years.

I got through to a secretary and let her know what had happened.

"I'll be sure to let Mr. Spencer know," she said, "and have him call you."

I thanked her and hung up. It wasn't what I wanted to hear. I wanted to talk to my attorney and find out if I could go over to Gram's. I needed to get over there and handle something that had belonged to Marty. Morgan would tell me what had been hers. He was used to Gram looking for odd objects and then giving them to me as I grew up.

I paced around the house a little bit, trying to be quiet. I debated unpacking, knowing that if I did, I'd end up just having to pack it up again. Of course, chances were if I didn't unpack, I wouldn't be allowed to move back in.

I heard my mom starting to move around in her bedroom just as my phone rang. I picked it up quickly, wishing I had thought to put it on vibrate.

"Ashley." It was Nick Spencer. He immediately gave me condolences on Marty.

"I'm wondering what that means for me?" I asked.

"At this point things are on hold, however, I'll prepare a motion to remove the injunction on you living in the carriage house. Once the murderer is found and charged, the challenge will disappear. In fact, the only reason anything remains is because you were questioned by the police not just about Martina's murder but about the murder of the police officer."

"Am I suspect?" I asked.

"Not so far as I can tell," Nick said. "They used the term 'person of interest' but I expect that they are very interested in you. You have something like an alibi from a number of different people that makes it hard for you to have killed your cousin. The same can't be said for Claire Wilcox, unfortunately. However, your father is equally suspect and at some point they might start questioning him."

"And he's one of my alibis for the time Marty was murdered," I said.

"Which is the problem. Despite that, if you'd like to go over to the house, that shouldn't be a problem. So long as Morgan is there to verify that you didn't take anything out of the house, it should be fine. If you need a recommendation for a criminal attorney, I know two who might work well for you."

Great, even my lawyer thought I might need representation.

"Should I call someone now before they say I'm a suspect or should I wait?" I asked.

Spencer went on about the pros and cons but, of course, he said, he was biased and would always recommend representation. Moments after we hung up he texted me the names and phone numbers of his criminal attorney recommendations.

"Who was that?" my mom asked sleepily. Her brown hair was mussed and not combed into the perfect little bob she normally had. She's about half an inch shorter than I am and about two sizes larger, pushing her to feel that she's fat, though I think she looks like Mom.

"Nick Spencer," I said. "I called him about the carriage house. I guess he's talking to a judge about removing the injunction against me living there. He said I could go over there so long as Morgan was around. I might do that."

Mom nodded.

"He gave me the name of a couple of attorneys who work criminal cases as well." I waited for her to react.

I expected my mom to stand up for me much in the way Aunt Daisy had. Instead she seemed to deflate.

"I just don't know," she muttered, stopping.

I wanted to jump and scream. How could she believe that she'd raised a child who could murder someone else? And not just anyone, but a person in their own family? A look at my face must have revealed what I was thinking.

"Not whether you could kill Marty or that policewoman, but I just don't know what life is coming to. I mean, first Marty challenges the will when she knew all along that you were Gram's primary beneficiary. Then she dies and so does that policewoman she was friends with. I worry."

I nodded, giving my mom a hug.

"Have you talked to Rick since you've been home? I'd feel better if you were with him when you aren't here. I like Cheri and all, but she's not going to be able to protect you if someone comes after you, too."

I tried not to shudder. Like I wanted to spend any more time than I had to with Rick.

"I'll be fine," I said. I went to grab my purse. "I'm just going to head over and talk to Morgan, okay? Are you okay?"

Mom nodded. "I'm going to grab some of that coffee you made and maybe play some mindless game on the computer for a few hours before I go back to Daisy's. We'll be going into the funeral home to set up Marty's funeral. I guess the police are releasing her body today."

"I'm sorry," I said. "Do you want me to come, too, or will you be okay?"

Mom shook her head. "You go and do your stuff. I'm sure another opinion will just mean we argue more over how Marty might have liked to be buried."

I looked back at my mom as I walked out the front door. She looked older than she had Saturday morning when I'd brought my stuff over. The last two days had taken a toll on her. I hated to see that. I needed to know who had murdered Marty if not for myself, then for my mom. I wasn't sure she was up to seeing me put on trial if the police decided to focus on me. Worse, what if they focused on me and my dad together? The permutations of that concept flew through my mind quickly and I shuddered as I hurried out into the already humid morning air.

Chapter 14

Gram's house sits at the end of a long drive that feels almost like a road. Just after turning into the drive, there's a large black gate that attaches to two red brick pillars that link up to the black split rail fence which lines the entire property. The pastures are demarcated by more split rail fence, always painted black, which seems traditional. Old hand-laid flat stone fences lined the property nearest the road, but much of that had sunk over the decades, so we didn't rely on it, except as part of the scenery.

I have a remote that I push to open the gate, which sits two car lengths back in a wide enough drive that someone without access could easily turn around. The horse boarders have their own gated entrance about a half mile down the road.

They don't have remotes, but that gate is open during the day and they have a code to get in after hours. Their turn around even has a small pull-out parking area if they need to search for something.

Pin oaks line the drive to the house, which is half a mile from the street. It was all done in concrete, which must have cost a fortune every time it needed to be redone. Across the fields there were sassafras trees, more oaks, a few sugar maples, and even a couple of pines.

Gram loved crepe myrtles, and there were three of those around the back of the house, near the carriage house.

The big house was a long two-story brick house in an old federalist style with tall white columns holding up a front porch for the full two stories. Symmetrical windows on either side lined the place, three on each side, also lined in white along with the shutters, giving a stark contrast to the dark red and black brick that the covered the house.

It was graceful and Gram and not at all me, which was why I always preferred the carriage house. There was a wing out the back to the left that wasn't visible that was considered one and half stories with more bedrooms and a loft. The loft had once been a place for me, Marty, and my brother to all play when it rained.

The loft had dormer windows which gave us tons of great hiding places. I don't think anyone ever used it much for anything now. I think Gram always expected that one of us would have kids and they'd play there. For the moment, my brother was the only one even married and he lived five hundred miles away.

Penelope Blue greeted me as I stepped out of the car. I saw her as a chocolate point Siamese that I could have reached down and petted but for the fact that my hand couldn't quite touch her. She rubbed her ghost self against my legs, happy that I was back. I was happy to be back, too. I wasn't pleased with the chill she always brought with her, the one that made my shin bone ache just a little, but seeing Penelope Blue always made me feel I was home.

Morgan wasn't far behind her in greeting me.

"No lawyer?" he asked. I was by the side door standing on the concrete stoop. I could look across the drive until it wound around beyond my carriage house. A garage was back there for the cars.

I shook my head. "Mr. Spencer told me I could come here if you supervised. He's going to try and get the injunction against me living in the carriage house thrown out."

Morgan smiled. "Well, that's one good thing. Get in here. I'll have Win fix you a good lunch."

I almost demurred, but my stomach growled. I

figured waiting for Win to make lunch would give me time to pace around and touch things that might give me clues to Marty's death.

Morgan didn't exactly do the supervising thing. He went to the right towards the large kitchen, which was not industrial but merely enormous. It was completely residential and decorated when Tuscan style kitchens were all the rage. Gram had used terra cotta tiles as a backsplash. The floor tiles blended nicely, and the granite counters had flecks of the same pinkish brown. Of course the stove had a huge brushed bronze fan and behind the stove were decorative tiles inset into the backsplash that rose to the ceiling.

Gram had mentioned being tired of it, though she had loved it fifteen years ago when she'd put it in. Then it had been new and unique. She was thinking of a more minimalist kitchen, not only because that was the fashion, but because it would be harder to tire of.

"I can always have wood cupboards repainted or stained and the wall tiles can be changed. If I got a plainer quartz, I could just redo the backsplash and paint the walls," she told me when I came home for Christmas, which was before we all knew she was dying.

I paused, looking through the arch to the kitchen, thinking about her, missing her. The smell of the big house was that unique scent that always reminded me of where I was, just like Penelope Blue. When Gram was alive, she'd have been in the great room that connected to the kitchen, probably reading a book at this time of the day. Sometimes on particularly nice days she might go visit the horses. It'd been a decade since she'd had her own horse, but she often went to make sure the horses that boarded with us were being treated well. Gram was something of a perfectionist, particularly about animals.

I headed into her study at the front of the house and looked around. This was where she had always done the bills. She had a computer set up with an ergonomic chair. The wall across from the door was lined with bookshelves in light maple wood. The desk was the same color as the shelves and was a smallish angled desk. She'd had a back built onto it so cords could run down to the floor, where she'd had an outlet installed, and not be seen by anyone.

A large window with a window seat was next to her desk. The room was painted a pale turquoise and the rug was a Persian type design with a background color that nearly matched the walls with flecks of green and pink and cream. The cushion on the window seat where generations of Gram's cats had snoozed as she worked, first by hand and then by computer, held the same colors.

Hellspark and Babs, Gram's two living chocolate point Siamese, were snoozing on the window seat. Hellspark glared at me from his place but did not move to come demand affection. You might think it odd that my Gram named a cat Hellspark. She was going through a Janet Kagan phase and loved the book of the same name. And Parkour, as we sometimes called him due to his activity level, lived up to the name when he was younger. For now, he looked content on the window seat. Morgan was probably slathering attention on them, feeling that he had to do something to assuage the cats' grief. Babs had always been less affectionate with anyone but Gram. I wondered how she was doing. She barely gave me a look when I came in.

There were photos on the walls without shelves, mostly family. I went to those.

The first was a picture of me and Marty when we were ten. I let my fingers brush across that one, knowing the types of memories that would come with it. I'd often used that photo to practice my psychic reactions and let Gram help me keep them in check.

I got plenty of my memories, of playing outside with Marty, riding horses with Marty and Gram, swimming in the pool that sat on the far side of the house from the carriage house, completely fenced with a view across the rolling hills down towards the pond where the horses could rest if they were out for the afternoon.

I remembered the time Marty had pushed me under the water and held me there until Gram came and rescued me. As always, I felt my lungs pounding as I struggled. I felt the anxiety that quickly turned to terror when I couldn't get my head out of the water. I felt the anger that I felt as a young adult as I came to realize what could have happened to my little girl self. I also felt Marty's shame at what she had done when she came to realize what could have happened.

Gram had made her touch the picture often as well, particularly when she was upset.

Marty's memories started flooding me. She'd been happy to hear I was coming. I felt her joy and saw an image of her and Gram talking about me returning to Kentucky.

I felt her accept Gram's explanation of the bequest, which didn't include Marty learning about my psychic abilities, something I had requested Gram not do, not after my mom's reaction. While I had chanced telling my friend Lisa back in Portland, I hadn't told anyone else.

Lisa had been my best friend in acupuncture school and she kept my secret, as I knew she would. She also hadn't judged me. She had her own gifts and was confident in them, so I didn't even have to deal with some misplaced jealousy about what I could do. The only time we'd worked with my gifts was when she couldn't find some class notes she needed for a test and her housemate wasn't around to let her use hers.

I longed for that sort of acceptance and connection, but I had a feeling I wasn't likely to find it in Kentucky. And so, even as an adult, even as a successful healer who sometimes used her abilities, asking to look at a favorite necklace or letting my psychic impressions work when I touched a driver's license or insurance card, I didn't tell anyone here.

I realized as I stood there, I was still afraid of what people would think.

This picture of Marty had nothing to tell me because she hadn't touched it after Gram died. She wouldn't have, probably. I needed something more personal.

I listened to Win in the kitchen and knew it would be a bit before she had something to offer me. I climbed the stairs, which were just around the corner from the study, and went to the second floor.

I headed towards the front corner bedroom Marty had claimed when she stayed at Gram's. It had windows on two walls and was always bright and pretty. We each had bedrooms we used when we stayed. I hadn't used mine in years, though I had moved the furthest and guested the most often. It was perhaps why I claimed the cottage. As a child, I had stayed in the front bedroom with the window seat, over Gram's study.

I glanced in to see that it had been done in deep soothing blues now, a very generic guest room. Penelope Blue showed up to give herself a bath in the window seat. She looked at me with her penetrating blue eyes and then went back to washing. She apparently approved of my mission. It was unusual to see her so often, and I couldn't help but think I had much to learn in the house.

I walked into Marty's room. It was still done in pinks and lavenders. The walls had light sponge painting, pale pinks against paler pinks. The bedding was pink and lavender and the wood on the bedding was an espresso colored wood which was a stark contrast to everything else.

Clothes were scattered on the bed and when I peeked in the dresser I saw more. I knew Marty had been at the house when Gram was dying, leaving only to go into work during Gram's last days. Marty hadn't immediately gone back to her apartment after, sticking around for family things. I hoped that whatever she'd touched with emotion might still be in the room.

I looked at her stuff, feeling strange to be searching my cousin's things when she was so recently gone, but at the same time reminding myself this was really the only way I could connect with her.

Penelope Blue showed up on the dresser and started playing with a pair of dangling earrings that held a dark stone at the bottom of their drop. I took the hint and fingered the gold chain of the earrings.

The cat settled in, watching me as I took in impressions.

I felt Marty being emotionally crushed by someone telling her she wasn't who they thought. I heard them but for some reason I couldn't see them. The voice was male and it felt like I had heard it before, though sometimes in a vision sound can get distorted. I tried not to focus on that.

I felt Marty turning to look back and I thought I got a glimpse of Detective Cabot but his face morphed into Landon Wright's. I remembered talking to Marty about Landon. She'd been heartbroken when they broke up. I felt that pain, that uncertainty.

There was anger, too, and the nearest I could sense was that the anger wasn't directed at Landon but at someone else. I wondered if Detective Cabot knew something. Why had he shown up in this memory of all memories? Was he there or was there another reason? Did Marty believe he'd said something to Landon?

I picked through the little information I had on Landon, mostly what I'd heard from Marty as I didn't know him other than by name. We'd grown up together and if I remembered right, he worked out at Toyota in Georgetown.

I got impressions of Marty laughing. There was a glass of champagne. I felt her pain upon losing Gram and her anger that Gram was dead. That was almost as overwhelming as my own pain. Her loss latched onto my own and I felt the hole open up in my chest, reaching down into my belly, tearing out anything I had inside.

I sank to my knees, letting go of the earring without even a second thought. Which was where Morgan found me when he came looking for me to make sure I had lunch.

Chapter 15

I ate while I talked to Morgan and Win about the house and what might be happening.

"If things go well and I can move into the carriage house, I'll ask Aunt Daisy if she wants to move in here. I know my folks don't want to," I said. If my parents needed to stay at the big house when they remodeled the kitchen, it was certainly large enough to accommodate them too.

"We'd love to have her," Morgan said. "Of course, I think we need all of you here. The house is too big to be so empty." He was wiping down the countertop. Win was washing dishes by hand, though there was a high-end dishwasher under the counter. Her wavy dark hair moved in time to the rhythm of the song she hummed, something that reminded me of salsa music. She was a lovely young woman, particularly when she wore bright colors, though she tended to favor bland clothing that I think she felt let her blend in. Seales, like so much of Kentucky, tends to be very white, and Win's Latin heritage often made her stand out more than she liked.

I enjoyed the frittata Win had whipped up, the smells of onions and green peppers tickling my nose. I liked the way she'd dipped the bread in the egg batter for a few minutes to make sure it stayed soft while the frittata had baked.

"Aunt Daisy talked about opening a bed and breakfast once," I said. "I have no idea if that's still an interest of hers but if it is, she could do it with this place."

"You wouldn't mind?" Win asked. "All your Gram's things and stuff?"

"We'd keep an area for Daisy and maybe cordon it off. Between that and the carriage house, we'd have plenty of places to keep personal items."

Win nodded, looking less than certain. Maybe it was the extra work, although she'd never acted as if she hated the work. In fact, though she was my age, I think she dug in and worked harder than I ever did. She really put me to shame.

"We could remodel that attic if it went well," Morgan was saying. "There's probably a computer program that would analyze when we were busiest and when we weren't and we could plan to remodel during a quiet time. At one time, I think that space could have been servant's quarters, though no one has used it in forever."

"I didn't think the house was that old." I hated to talk through a mouthful of frittata, but I did.

"Not many people had servants that lived in still, then," Morgan said, "but a few did. And the plans were for a house with servant's quarters upstairs. Miz Beauvoir said that they'd planned to finish them if they were needed, but they never were. As you know, Win and I have rooms at the far end of the house."

I nodded. I didn't like to think of moving Morgan and Win upstairs, but perhaps we'd have to if Daisy moved in and we did the B&B thing. Or maybe we'd just do a more informal type of rental property. I didn't have to decide right away, and it would all be up to Daisy if she wanted to do something like that.

"You've thought about this," I said.

"Miz Daisy talked about it for a few years, tried to talk your Gram into it." Morgan put away the cloth he was using to wipe the counters and straightened. "It stopped though, so maybe she's not so interested in that any longer."

"I doubt she's interested in much at all, now," Win added. She was drying a pan and handing it off to Morgan.

"Sometimes a good project is just what you need to take your mind off your sorrows," Morgan said easily.

I wasn't at all sure setting up a B&B was what would take Daisy's mind off of losing her daughter, but I didn't say that. Morgan was just talking. He liked talking and I liked listening. No need to remind him of his own sorrows, or have him and Win pouring over mine.

Instead I finished my lunch and went to the study to call Cheri.

"How are you?" Cheri asked without even a greeting.

"I'm okay," I said. "Mr. Spencer said I could come back to Gram's at least for a visit. He's hoping to get the injunction against my living in the carriage house reversed today."

"I should hope so," Cheri said. "How is your aunt? My mama went over there yesterday afternoon and she said that she's just broken, not herself at all. As if you could expect anything else after what happened. That LeAnn was there, too, Mama said, and seemed to be glowering at Daisy. Your mom was just as nice to LeAnn as could be, though Mama thought she should have ripped LeAnn a new one and you know Mama doesn't talk like that!"

I shared a laugh with Cheri, picturing her mother saying that. Stacy Price was a rather formal, prim woman who took her church-going a little too seriously. Cheri hadn't been allowed to date boys until sixteen, even to go out with a group. Stacy tended to be judgmental about anything she didn't understand, nor did she drink alcohol. The idea that she said "rip her a new one" about LeAnn spoke volumes.

"I remembered that Marty used to date Landon Wright, but you said he wasn't in town, right?" I asked.

"Right," Cheri said. "We all know that because that would be the first thing the police looked for because of how recently they'd broken up. Everyone said Landon did the breaking up, but you never know. He might have just said that to keep his pride, you know?"

I agreed. I did know.

"But I think it was for real. I remember Marty was pretty broken up and then you came home which seemed to make it easier for her—you know, she had something else to focus on," Cheri said. "Now that she's gone, I know Landon is pretty ripped apart too. I mean, they didn't exactly end on good terms. I guess the breakup was pretty ugly and rumor has it he was saying Marty had changed and he wondered if whatever had made her change led to her murder."

"Like could she have been taking drugs?" I asked.

"I don't think it was that," Cheri said, "at least that's not what's been intimated to me. I think it was more that she had other interests and was becoming someone he didn't like very much. I guess that could be drugs, but it just wasn't Marty, you know? She'd be more the type to just take a drink because it wasn't expensive and it was easy. If we had legal pot, maybe she'd have used some of that, mostly because that would be easy too. Anything harder would have required she go find someone to sell it to her and she didn't have the interest."

That sounded a lot like my cousin. If she was going to do something illegal, it would have been something that cut corners, not something that she had to go out and find.

"Do you know if Marty knew Detective Cabot?" I asked.

"Why?" Cheri returned.

It was the question I was dreading. I couldn't tell her how I knew, after all, not without giving away my secret, but it seemed important, at least a little.

"It was just something about the way he talked, I guess," I said, hoping Cheri wouldn't take this as fact and actually answer my question.

"I haven't heard anything. I mean, it's a small town, so they might have seen each other, and she knew Claire Wilcox and Wilcox was on the force with Cabot," Cheri said slowly putting pieces together. "I heard that Wilcox wasn't especially well liked here, so I can't imagine that she and Cabot were good friends either. Do you suppose that he's behind things?"

I doubted that very much and I let Cheri know that. "I was just wondering. He and Officer Wilcox reacted so differently to Marty's death. I wasn't sure it was just that she knew Marty so well or not. In fact, when it first happened, I felt like Cabot knew Marty, not Wilcox." Which I realized was true. It made me wonder what was going on.

"I'll keep my ears open," Cheri said, which I knew meant she'd be asking questions here and there about what was going on. I didn't want to encourage her, but I really wanted to know. I hadn't been here enough for a very long time to know what was what. Cheri had told me what she thought was important, but maybe she knew things that she didn't think were important. Someone else might bring those things up.

When I finally hung up, I looked around the study. I'd sat in the club chair that was in the corner and faced the window seat. Penelope Blue was there now, stretching out as if she were enjoying the sunshine. It surprised me because Hellspark and Babs had been there earlier. I wondered where they'd wandered off to.

Penelope Blue noticed I was off the phone and

she came over to sit on my lap, her tiny ghost paws gliding over the top of the carpet as she leaped up easily.

That was unusual. Normally she'd just watch me and maybe get into something to draw my attention to it, but she never stepped on me. Her paws were cool but not the icy cold I had expected from a ghost. She didn't really have a weight but more like a slight pressure, as if there was almost something there.

"What is it?" I asked. I reached my hand out to touch her, wondering if she could feel me petting her.

"Meow," Penelope Blue said, her Siamese voice echoing in my ears.

I went through the motions of rubbing her back, though I couldn't feel anything. My hand grew a bit cool but, again, not cold. She gave me a satisfied look and then leaped off of me and wandered out of the room.

Did she miss Gram?

I hurried out of the room and went up the stairs. Gram had had a bed put in the formal living room downstairs before she died, but most of her life she'd had a bedroom upstairs. I didn't doubt that Penelope Blue was leading me there. Morgan didn't appear to be around, for which I was grateful, no matter that he was supposed to supervise me. Win was in the great room dusting around the fireplace, and she gave me a quick smile when she noticed me looking.

Penelope turned left at the top of the stairs and then slipped through the door to Gram's bedroom. I followed.

The room brought back memories, the large king-sized bed against the far wall off to the left of the doorway still covered in green and brown brocade. The walls were done in an old-fashioned floral wallpaper that Gram had never changed.

"Eddie liked it and helped me chose it. He never liked change the way I did, so it always stayed. Now that he's gone, I can't bear to remove something he loved," she'd said more than once as the master bedroom became more and more outdated.

She'd certainly changed the bathroom, removing the original sitting area and making it a large master en suite bathroom with a whirlpool tub and a walk-in shower that held a bench before that became fashionable. The old bathroom that had sat in a corner off the bedroom with just a toilet, shower and sink, got opened up into a walk-in closet.

But the bedroom, the bedroom proper had stayed the same. The floor was still old, thin planked hardwood with a pine colored stain and the rug covering it was still a faded green that I remembered from my childhood. Even then the rug had looked faded and old. Only the covers on the bed ever changed, but the colors on them had stayed the same, pulling together the colors of the wallpaper.

The curtains were open and the blinds that had been hung beneath them were up, letting plenty of light into the room, contrasting against the latte-colored wood of the bed frame, dresser, and dressing table. There was a bench under the window which sat across from the door, and that was covered in a green needlepoint print which looked like something a medieval woman would have done.

Hellspark looked up at me and meowed. I noted a rounded lump in the middle of the bed, under the covers, that was likely Babs. I went over and rubbed Hellspark' head, enjoying the feel of his short, plush fur. He gave me a small purr and began to knead his paws against the bench. I looked around the room, wondering what Penelope Blue had brought me to look at.

The dressing table caught my eye. It held Gram's jewelry box, a small white box that wasn't even very fancy. She had a larger, free-standing one in the walk-in closet, but this little box kept the jewelry she loved. I had put her wedding ring in the safe.

I walked over and opened the white box, noting the faded red floral print, and thought about how it must have stood out when the colors were still bright. Thinking that and running my fingers over it, I could see it, the flowers blooming in the green room like the first hint of spring in a garden.

I felt Gram's pride in how that looked and her love of the jewelry box, which had been given to her by my grandfather on her birthday just about a month after their engagement.

Inside were the pearl earrings she wore to any slightly fancy gathering. I touched one and was overwhelmed with her feelings, the worry about getting older, a sense that something wasn't right with her body, her sadness at not seeing me married, the joy of knowing she'd see Eddie, my grandfather, again.

Tears reached the corners of my eyes, though I wasn't hollowed out with sorrow. There was equal joy and anticipation when she'd worn these earrings, so the sorrow was more my own at all the feelings over the years, drawing me back with them.

I saw the world through her eyes, first my brother graduating from high school, then Marty, and finally me. I saw my brother getting married and the way she saw his wife as being perfect for him. She'd touched my sister-in-law's hand with the engagement ring on it and she felt the love and joy and got a sense that it was solid and lasting. Gram had so much more talent than I did.

Standing there I wished to see my grandmother, tears falling, though I smiled. I turned, still holding the earring, to see a young woman sitting on the bed, her head cocked and her mouth open in surprise.

Chapter 16

"Who are you?" I asked, realizing the answer even as Penelope Blue leaped on the girl's lap.

The surprise faded, and the young woman petted the cat, no longer looking at me. I wondered if she could even see me.

"I can see you," she said, her voice like my mom's, but stronger, more confident. The tone surprised me. There was a hint of gravel in the voice too, a sexy kind of thing that movie stars in the fifties made popular. I recalled that Gram had always had that hint, but I'd never really thought she sounded like my mom all that much.

"Gram?" I asked.

"If I am, it certainly hasn't happened yet," the young woman laughed.

"Do you know what happens later in your life? Are you a ghost?" I asked, wondering. Penelope Blue seemed content with her. She didn't seem to see me or notice me at all.

"No," Young Gram said. "Are you?"

"I'm Ash. Ashley Jericho, your granddaughter." I didn't want to tell her what year it was, hated that she could see me looking as I did. I wished it happened longer after death, so that she wouldn't have a hint of when she'd die.

"And if you think I'm a ghost, I must be dead by your time, am I right?" Now Gram sounded exactly like Gram.

I nodded, not sure what to say.

"You look disappointed."

"I guess I was hoping that I could go to you for answers about something that's happened," I said, "like I always did. You understood about being psychic and knowing things. I was hoping you could help."

"Ghosts are funny," Gram said. I was getting used to seeing her as a pretty girl. "I've seen horses and cats and sometimes I saw my grandfather in his home after he died. He never spoke, of course, and he never saw me the way the animals did. I think sometimes it's harder for people. If they are ghosts, they're so caught up in their own things that they don't realize that they can talk to people. Even if they can, I sometimes wonder if it's hard or something. My mom talked about trying to talk to her great-grandmother, but she seemed to come from so far away. They were never quite able to communicate."

"You never told me," I said.

"Maybe because I didn't want to limit what potential you might have. Maybe we had this conversation and I knew you'd be looking for me, and I wanted you to have the hope of doing so," Gram said. She looked down at Penelope Blue and petted her again. "I'm sure there will be a good reason even if I don't know it now."

That made sense. Penelope Blue leaped off of Gram's lap and into the room with me. At the moment the cat left her lap, Gram disappeared, and it was just me and Penelope Blue in the room, or rather me and Penelope Blue's ghost.

Leaning back against the dresser, I wondered if I touched something else if I'd see Gram again, perhaps looking forward in time. How much had she really known?

I wished I could see the woman I had known as Gram in the way I had known her so I could ask her about what was going on and get her insights, but clearly that avenue was closed to me.

After a few minutes of wandering around, letting my hands brush against items, some of which brought strong emotions, others of which gave me memories of Gram's life, I left the room. Penelope Blue was settled on the bed and appeared to be snoozing. Did ghost cats need to snooze?

The lump that was Babs was still there. If she'd felt the young woman who had appeared, she'd not bothered to move. I wondered what the cats thought of Penelope Blue. I rarely saw her with them.

Walking down the stairs to the main level where Morgan and Win were talking in the kitchen, I wondered about the differences in human ghosts and non-human ghosts. Why would cats and dogs be able to interact with us and ghost humans couldn't? It troubled me. Was it just that humans were so eager to be off?

I paused at the bottom of the stairs and then headed towards the front room, the formal living area where Gram had had a bed for the last weeks of her life because she couldn't climb the stairs.

The room was done in creams and yellows with splashes of pale green in throw pillows and the curtains. The room had white wainscoting halfway up the walls and the palest yellow paint. No wallpaper lined the walls to make them busy.

"It's a cold, formal room," Gram had said, "dated though it is. I wish there was space in my study to put a bed."

There would have been had she really wanted

it. The desk could have been moved and the chairs, but she didn't want people to go to all that trouble. Instead she'd spent her last weeks in the formal room, though we had brought in colorful blankets.

The pictures on the walls were old-fashioned prints of horses on hunts with dogs running. I suspected that nothing had been changed because my grandfather had liked those. The pictures were such that they would have made a room any other color quite dark. The only time we used the formal living room was when Gram had her holiday party. The party used the whole house, but sometimes guests mingled in the living room. Usually she had a Christmas tree in there with a few presents for acquaintances and people who worked around the house, assuming she hadn't already adopted them as family.

The tree would be done in gold and blue, and the presents wrapped in shiny foils. The main tree would always be in the great room. It was decorated with a hodgepodge of ornaments in every color of the rainbow, often made by kids at some point. Gram also had a lot of collectible and souvenir ornaments that people had given her over time. She'd even collected a few herself.

I wasn't sure what had drawn me to the living room, but I felt I needed to be in there. I walked in and stared out the window, over the green lawn and the bushes that kept the house slightly hidden from the road.

I shook my head. This was mine now, though I had no idea what I'd do with it. Maybe someday I could live there, if I had a family, but even then it seemed too big. It had always suited Gram. It seemed right for us to come visit, but as her life had started coming to an end, it had suddenly become overwhelmingly large, a burden I was going to have to take on alone, much like my psychic abilities.

"You know the real reason I couldn't see human ghosts?" I heard the voice in my head and around the room. I whirled, heart thudding, looking.

There she sat in the formal sofa, Gram, looking as she had most of my life, with her white hair and classy slacks and a sweater. She had on soft slippers, the pearl earrings I'd just been fingering, and a gold necklace of the sort she often wore.

"Why?" I asked, barely breathing the word, hoping Morgan wouldn't show up wondering who I was talking to.

"I was always afraid of what they might tell me," Gram said.

It stunned me, both the simplicity of the answer and her admitting she was afraid.

"But you're not me, clearly, and so here we

are. You've been thinking of me and you need something. What is it?"

My mouth dropped open as I wondered where I could even begin.

Chapter 17

Gram was sitting on the sofa, which was cream, in the left corner with the cream and green pillows edged with pale gold piping. If it had been any darker, the room would have looked even more dated. As it was, it looked familiar. She was waiting for me to respond. I smelled the faint traces of gardenia, a scent she'd worn when I was younger.

Penelope Blue leaped up onto her lap and turned around several times before settling in, just as if she were a real cat on a real lap instead of just a ghost of a cat who had lived a long time ago.

I backed up, feeling suddenly strange, sort of scared, because while I could see ghost cats, seeing a ghost human wasn't something that had happened to me before. It was strange the way seeing a person I had known changed my attitude about ghosts and made me more fearful.

"Gram?" I whispered. It was a stupid thing to do, I know.

"I thought that was clear," she said. "Am I not clear?"

"You're clear," I said. "I think I'm not clear. I'm just in shock."

She nodded as if it all made sense to her.

"Did you know about Marty?" I asked.

"I do," she said.

"Can you help me find who killed her? I'm a person of interest and her friend Officer, er I mean, Claire, Wilcox has died too." I kept my voice soft, always worried that Morgan would come in or hear my side of the conversation. Then I realized that having him walk in wouldn't be the worst—he was used to Gram and I doing weird things. If Win came in, she might just flee if she had a clue I thought I was talking to Gram.

"That woman was a piece of work," Gram said, referring to Claire Wilcox, not Win. "I didn't know about her, but there was no reason for me to do so. She was always pushing her ideas onto Marty. Of course, Marty being Marty, would start parroting back whatever that woman thought. I tried to put my foot down, but I wasn't at my best."

Of course not.

"Do you know anyone who would have killed Marty?"

"It would depend upon what the Wilcox woman told her to do or say, don't you think?" Gram said. "Or maybe Marty got some other weird ideas somewhere. I was sorry when she broke up with that Landon fellow. He was a nice young man, probably too nice for her."

So Gram had known that. And she'd liked Landon.

"Not like that Rick. I have never been so glad to hear you'd broken up with someone. He was bad news, and, from my perspective now, he still is, so you're well rid of him."

I shuddered. "I ran into him downtown the other day. He's as weird as ever. He seemed nice when we started going out."

"We all live and learn, don't we?" Gram said. "It's why there's life, after all, to learn interesting things and try on new ways of being."

I wondered if that was a veiled reference to a meaning of life speech. I wasn't sure I was ready to get all esoteric with Gram.

"But Marty?" I asked, bringing Gram back to the focus.

"She had a big fight with your friend Cheri Price shortly before you came back. I guess Marty didn't think Cheri needed to immediately call you.

Marty wanted to talk to you first, though I can't say what that was about. Apparently it's not something I need to know. That's sort of how things are here."

"Cheri?" I asked, feeling as if someone had kicked me.

"Clearly you've far more fortitude for the truth than I ever had," Gram said. "I expected your mind to kick me out at that revelation."

"But it's true?" I pressed.

"Cross my heart," Gram said. She smiled and then looked sad all in the course of one of my heartbeats.

I hated to think that about Cheri, but I was going to have to start investigating her, too. I wasn't sure who to go to. If Rick wasn't so untrustworthy, I'd go to him. I just couldn't bear to think about having to do that. Still, I couldn't think why Cheri would kill Marty and then Officer Wilcox.

"But to kill Marty?" I said. "And why Officer Wilcox?"

Gram shrugged. "Or maybe that's the point. Maybe that Wilcox woman killed Marty and Cheri suspected, so she took it into her own hands. I just can't see it though, can you? But I bet she might know something. Talk to her about that conversation."

"I will."

Gram nodded. She started to fade, rather like a fog dissipating.

"Thank you," I told her, hoping she'd come back. When she was gone, Penelope Blue was still snoozing, about the height of Gram's leg, just above the sofa. She gave me a glare and stood up, stretching and then turned and sat on the actual sofa, or as close to as ghosts get.

Chapter 18

I wandered out of the room and looked in the kitchen. Win wasn't around. I went out the side door to my car. Morgan was on the stoop, sitting on the step. Normally he remained standing.

"What's up?" I asked.

"Takin' a rest," he said, smiling a little and standing. "I'm getting old. It's funny how that sneaks up on you, isn't it?"

I agreed that it was. He stood to one side so I could get to my car.

"I'll air out the carriage house for you," he said. "I expect that the judge will be throwing out the challenge to the will. Daisy won't be picking it up. Heard her around here the day Marty filed it. She was not happy with her daughter." He gave me a knowing nod.

"Thanks, Morgan. I don't think the carriage house has been closed up for long enough to need an airing out."

"Keeps me from having to go upstairs and do those rooms, though," he laughed. "Like I said, getting old." Again that turn and head shaking.

I got in the car and waved at him, feeling sad. First, I had to see my Gram as a ghost and have her tell me my best friend had kept a falling out with my cousin from me. Then Morgan was reminding me that he, too, was getting old. As if I could imagine the house without him. His presence there was such that when we lost him, it would be every bit as hard as losing Gram.

In her will, she'd stipulated that he could retire in the house. He had family around, and I knew he wouldn't leave the area, so likely he'd only leave if he wanted to be on his own. He could also go if he thought he was being a burden, something I knew I'd have to talk him out of.

I considered calling Cheri right then, but I didn't want to have the conversation while I was driving. The sun was high in the afternoon sky. The day was bright and the skies were dark blue, though in the distance I saw some dark gray clouds. Probably a thunderstorm later on.

I was turning onto my parent's street when the phone rang. I slowed, hitting the button on my dash to answer the call, watching carefully as seven-year-old Cora Schneider from up the road was out on her bike. She must be visiting her grandparents and was riding alongside the street. I didn't want her to inadvertently turn into traffic as I hurried by.

She waved seeing the car and I waved back. She wasn't old enough to remember me and my visits regularly, but clearly she was a friendly child. I waved at Mrs. Schneider, her grandmother, who was standing at the end of the driveway. I marveled that her hair was dark brown and her face appeared unlined or barely more so than mine. Her chin was thickening compared to the thin woman I remembered, but other than that she was ramrod straight and as hearty as ever.

I didn't remember Gram ever looking that young, but maybe it was just my memories of her that didn't let me remember her that way.

"This is Ash," I said into the phone when I finally answered.

"Nick Spencer," the voice came on. "You are clear to move into the carriage house. The challenge hasn't completely gone away, but it's on hold pending the outcome of the murder investigation. Once you've been fully cleared by the police, and you're well on your way there, the challenge will go away."

"That's wonderful," I said, already thinking about how I was going to have to move all my stuff back to the house. Maybe I'd leave some of it until the weekend when my dad could help me. Or maybe I'd find someone to help me move boxes. I considered who I knew in town that I wouldn't mind asking for that kind of help. I had avoided asking for it when Marty forced me out, simply because I didn't want to put someone in an awkward position of feeling as if they were taking sides.

I pulled into the driveway still thinking about who I could call. My friend, Eric Hunt, was around. He'd gone to UK, making the commute from home. He worked in accounting and now ran his own place downtown. He'd gotten married a couple of years ago. We'd had a bunch of classes together, and for a long time he'd debated about going into medicine as well. In fact, his first year at UK we'd done the whole biology, wanna-go-pre-med thing together. We'd both mostly dropped it, though I'd ended up going off to acupuncture school while he'd gone into business.

Still, we were buddies. I'd heard about all his ups and downs with his wife, Chelsea, before they were husband and wife. I'd come out for the wedding though I had only stayed a couple of days. He and I had talked before Gram's death, but since her funeral, not so much. Chances were, he didn't know what to say. In typical Eric fashion, he was staying away.

He'd done that in school when he found our mutual friend Thad was gay. He hadn't known how to handle it, and so he'd stopped talking to him. I'd been the one in the middle. To this day, I don't think he and Thad talk too much. It was less about judgment that it was wrong and more about Eric not wanting to act badly, thus making him do exactly what he'd tried not to do.

I considered whether to call him and ask for help moving my stuff back this weekend or calling Cheri. Looking at the time, it was late. Cheri was at work and the end of the day was coming. Maybe I'd wait until she got home so she couldn't claim to be distracted while she figured out a way to not tell me what I needed to know. Cheri may talk a lot, but when she wants to keep a secret, she's very good at it.

My mom was gone. She hadn't left a note. I figured she was with Aunt Daisy. Having to go to the funeral home was probably very emotional for both of them. She hadn't called me to let me know, so she must not have felt she needed me to be there. I wasn't sure if I felt left out or if I was relieved. I'd never picked out a casket. Gram had planned her own funeral and prepaid for it, so there wasn't much to do. The closest I'd come to funeral planning was talking to patients who were going through the process. It gave me an idea about the decisions to be made but not personal connection to the decisions.

I wasn't terribly hungry after the frittata that Win had made up for me. I got some lemonade and sipped it, sitting at the little table in the eating nook, looking out the back. I wondered if I should pack my bags up or if it was better to stay here for one last night. If I went, I'd need to remake the bed in the carriage house as I'd used my own sheets, not Gram's.

I gave Morgan a quick call to let him know I'd be there the next day. He'd get things taken care of, probably have Win scrubbing the bathrooms, one of which was upstairs. He'd made it very clear he wasn't climbing stairs if he could avoid it.

The two of them would probably also plan to have some food on hand in case I got hungry. I didn't need them to do that, but Gram had always had them do it when I stayed, so it was part and parcel of living in the carriage house.

I heard my dad drive in. When he came through the garage he asked me how things were. I gave him an update, leaving out the part about needing to talk to Cheri.

"Your mom is staying at Daisy's again," he said. "I guess Daisy really fell apart at the funeral home. Fortunately, Pastor Francis had insisted upon coming along, so there was someone else there."

I was surprised to hear about the pastor. I didn't realize he normally helped people plan funerals. I wondered what was up with that. Maybe it was just all in day's work for a pastor, but I wasn't certain. He hadn't helped us plan Gram's funeral. Granted she'd done most of the choosing. Still, we'd had to go down on our own and sign papers and get things moving, picking a date for the viewing and the service and deciding if we were going to invite people to meet afterwards, which, of course, we did in Gram's house.

Maybe he was there because Marty was the second person our family had to bury in such a short time. Still, I had to wonder about his presence in Daisy's house and then helping with the funeral planning. Was he keeping an eye on her? Could he have been the one who killed Marty? I tried not to laugh at the image of Pastor Francis welding one of the large candlesticks on the altar and hitting Marty over the head with it. No. My real curiosity was if he and Daisy were maybe a couple, or perhaps heading that way.

I chatted with my dad and we decided to go out to grab some food at Seales Tavern and Grill. The Tavern sat up on a small hill, almost a bluff. When there was a lot of rain, sometimes there was a small stream at the bottom, but mostly it was just a small gorge, not much more than a ditch. In fact, I think in Oregon and Washington they called something like that a ditch. Here it was a viewpoint.

Seales Tavern and Grill did a good job with burgers, steaks, and pasta. They also did a pretty good pizza, if you went in for simple pizza with pepperoni or sausage. Nothing too fancy there. Still, I couldn't complain.

My dad and I spent some time talking about the move back to the carriage house. I hoped to sleep there the next evening. I told him I'd be calling a few friends to help load up boxes. My dad volunteered his truck to take them over, so long as he didn't have to carry them all out of the basement.

I agreed that he wouldn't. In fact, if I had to, I'd check on social media and hire a couple of guys with strong backs to load up the boxes. It wasn't as if I didn't have money. After dinner, when we'd gotten home and my dad was settling in to watch something on Netflix, I headed to my room to call Cheri. I couldn't put it off any longer.

Chapter 19

I flopped on my twin bed and stared up at the cream ceiling before calling Cheri. The ceiling wasn't plain. It wasn't that popcorn stuff, either. Instead it had low swirls on it. While my bed was comfortable enough, the mattress conforming to my body, still, after all these years, I was going to be glad to have the wider bed in the carriage house. Maybe I'd even get a cat. After all, if I decided to go away, I had Morgan and Win to take care of it. Or else my mother, though I worried if I did that, she'd adopt the thing while I was gone and I'd have to come over for visitation.

I had had a cat in college, after I'd moved out of the dorms. I had gone away for spring break with Cheri. We'd taken a long girls' weekend midweek, as Cheri liked to say, though it made no sense, and gone down to Beaufort, South Carolina. It wasn't quite Florida, but the weather was nice enough and we'd avoided the crowds of drunk kids our age. My mom had volunteered to cat sit and when I got back, my cat was missing.

I'd immediately called home, thinking that something horrible had happened, but my mom told me that Tony had been lonely and she'd taken him home. She'd felt that he needed more attention than I could give him as a student. We'd argued for a few weeks, but I'd eventually given in to my mother's arguments after seeing how pleased Tony was to be living in her house.

As far as cats went, it was certainly possible that Hellspark would take a liking to me and I could bring both Gram's Siamese out to the carriage house. I had no doubts that Babs would take some time to warm to me, but perhaps she'd eventually come around if I were the one feeding her.

After thinking about that longer than I needed to, smelling the lavender scent of Mom's laundry detergent, listening to the mumble of the show Dad was watching, I finally called Cheri.

"Hey there," she said. "I was thinking about you. Did you hear from Mr. Spencer?"

"I did. Set to move back tomorrow, although I'm going to call a few people to help move books back on the weekend. My dad is not up to carrying all those boxes back out of the basement so soon."

Cheri chattered on about who was around and who wasn't. She immediately thought of Eric and even Thad, though I doubted I needed both of them to help. Eric probably knew people in the area. I let her talk for a bit, wanting to ease into my confrontation.

"So I was asking around and I heard you and Marty had a falling out shortly before I came back," I said.

There was silence on the other end. I wondered what Cheri was thinking. Finally a sigh. "It wasn't exactly a falling out."

"What do you mean?"

"Once Marty started being friendly with Claire Wilcox, she got really confrontational about things. I mean, not all the time, mind you, just now and then so that it was always a surprise and you couldn't really expect it."

I waited, giving her some sounds to let her know I was there.

"You were coming home and she started yelling at me for seeing Rick Darlington a few times. We weren't dating, but he was lonely and sometimes we'd go out. He'd always ask about you, which I thought was weird if he was interested in me. I wasn't seeing anyone then," Cheri said. "You know, since Junior ran off with that slut, I've had a lot of confidence issues and all and it was nice to have some male company even if I wasn't ready to *date* date and really didn't want to date Rick."

The last was breathless. So this went back to Cheri's divorce and how she saw herself. But why would Marty have such an issue with Cheri seeing Rick?

"What was Marty's beef with Rick?" I asked. I mean, I knew my family didn't like him. And he'd been an ass when we'd been together but not like a dangerous ass that everyone had to stay away from. More an annoyance. It wasn't like Cheri would bring him to family gatherings or anything, either, so they wouldn't even have to see him.

"I heard that he went out with Claire a few times and he was hitting on Marty in front of her, and that just set Marty off. I think Claire was pretty upset about their breakup."

"I can't believe you didn't tell me. Maybe she was jealous and that's why she trying so hard to set me up as Marty's killer." I was kind of pissed off at Cheri. How could she not say anything? Of course, maybe that's what Marty's confrontation was about—not telling me about Rick and Claire.

"That's old news. I mean this was before you even came home. Besides, Marty made it very clear she thought I should let it go and not tell you. I wouldn't have listened if you didn't make it very clear what you thought of Rick."

I had, I knew. I was kind of a bitch about it, but he'd been a jerk himself. Neither of us had acted well.

"It would have been nice to know," I said. "And you're sure that Rick hadn't liked Marty or Claire enough to get jealous or anything and maybe kill her?"

"Can you really see him killing someone?" Cheri asked.

I had to admit it seemed farfetched. Rick was a brooder, not someone who acted on things, so the idea of him killing Marty in a fit of passion didn't really fit. He'd be more likely to sit in his home and seethe. Of course, weren't those the ones who snapped?

I shivered, unable to believe I was thinking that way.

Cheri moved onto other subjects and I was hanging up the phone when the doorbell rang.

I hurried to the door to see who it was. When I got to the hallway, I saw Detective Cabot in the entry of the house. He looked serious.

"I'd like to ask you a few questions," Cabot was saying to my father. I didn't even hear the rest. I was flying down the hallway.

"I thought you talked to him the other day. What other questions can you have?" I demanded.

Cabot looked startled by my question and then almost a little embarrassed. I'd always put him as being older than I was, but now, standing in this light, in our house, he seemed perhaps not so much older than I was but more worn. I remembered how he'd almost seemed tired when he'd interviewed me for the first time. What could have made him be so tired?

Suddenly all sorts of cop conspiracies ran through my mind.

I tried to pause my brain, reminding myself I was suspecting a cop, again. At least with Detective Wilcox there appeared to have been a reason for my suspicions. I couldn't think of one for Detective Cabot. Except for that one brief psychic image of him when I'd touched Marty's earrings.

"I need to follow up on a few things," Cabot said. His eyes held mine for a little too long, and I felt a flurry of what might have been desire stir. I tramped it down like a stray weed or tried to. Like so many weeds, it wasn't about to be pulled even if this wasn't the time, the place, or the appropriate guy.

I waited there.

"I'd like to talk with your father alone," he added.

My dad gave me a look and stepped out onto the porch with Detective Cabot. What was so important that he'd had to come here so late in the evening?

I considered trying to listen at the door but instead I paced around the living room, hoping that my dad was okay.

He came in, looking sad. Detective Cabot followed him and looked at me.

"I'd like to ask you a few questions as well," he said. "Alone."

So it was my turn to step outside and talk to him in the warm night air. At least it wasn't raining, though I heard thunder off in the distance.

Chapter 20

The sun had mostly set. I had to rely on the porch light which my dad must have turned on. It was light enough that shadows crawled across the lawn. A few frogs were out calling to one another and the cicadas had gone silent.

I smelled the faint traces of rain and the close feeling on my skin. It was going to rain soon, so I hoped that the questions Cabot was going to ask me went quickly.

Detective Byron Cabot—it took me a minute to remember his first name, I was so used to thinking of him as "Detective"—stared at me with his dark eyes for a minute before starting to speak. If I wasn't so worried that he was going to take me in because he believed I murdered Marty and Officer Wilcox, I'd have thought the look was sexy.

Instead, I thought back to mysteries I read and decided it was a trick to get me to speak.

Way to kill a moment. Not that there was a moment. Not that I wanted a moment. Or maybe I did. It had been a long time since Adam and I had broken up when I came home.

"I need you to go over with me where you were in the early hours of Saturday morning," he said.

I thought back to the day. I started with coming to my parents' house and later finding out that Marty had died. I worked backwards, talking about how I'd finished packing some of my personal belongings and hauled books out to the car. I'd stripped the bed at some point because I was taking my own sheets with me. Who knew how long I'd be gone?

"When did you learn about the challenge to the will?" he asked.

Again, it took me a moment to think. I asked to look at a calendar on his phone. I'd left mine in my room.

I said about a week earlier. Gram had died three weeks ago. The will had been read about ten days after that, after the funeral and after things had settled down. It could have been read sooner but no one really cared hearing about it. I know I didn't.

Marty had filed the challenge on a Thursday.

Mr. Spencer had challenged the challenge on Friday, which had asked that I be out of the carriage house that weekend. We got the next week for me to pack up my personal items and leave, with a stipulation that I had to have an inventory of anything I took out of the big house. Marty's attorney had wanted an inventory of everything taken out of the carriage house as well.

The judge had sided with Mr. Spencer. I had heard about the challenge on Thursday.

"How well did you know your cousin?" Cabot asked, switching things up.

"I thought pretty well," I said honestly. "But I didn't see this coming. Gram had talked about the will now and then, so I knew that I'd inherit the house and enough money to make sure I wouldn't have a problem paying someone to help me take care of it. I really prefer the carriage house and I had planned to ask my Aunt Daisy, Marty's mother, if she wanted to live in the big house. Marty could have too, if she'd wanted."

Cabot made a note. "Were you hurt by the challenge?"

"More confused," I said. "I had an acupuncture practice back in Washington State, just over the border from Portland. I sold it when I knew Gram was dying because I knew she wanted me to have the house and not just to sell. There'd be issues with that given the bequests to Morgan and even to Win that depend upon someone in the family owning the house. I had expected that I'd split the shares of the bourbon business with the family, which I did."

"What would you have done if Marty had won?"

"I guess I hadn't even thought about that. I'd already been planning on restarting my business here. I applied for a license though that hasn't come through. I've poked around a bit for office space. I guess I'd have stayed and found a place to live that's not my old bedroom."

Cabot nodded. "So you didn't worry about where you'd live or how your life might have gone?"

I shook my head.

"Did you know your cousin well enough to have thought of who might have done this?" Cabot asked.

I shook my head. "I wish I did. Marty was spending a lot of time with people I didn't know. I found out the other day that one of them was Officer Wilcox, but that's all I know. She broke up with her boyfriend, Landon, before Gram died. I don't know that they had much contact."

"Did you know Landon?"

"Some," I said. "It's a small town." Which surprised me that I didn't know Detective Cabot at all, didn't remember him from school or anyone talking about him. In fact, even Cheri didn't seem to know much about him.

He nodded and indicated that I should go on.

"I guess a lot of the family liked him. He treated Marty well. From what I heard, though, he broke up with her."

"Do you think he could have killed her?"

"I can't imagine why he would have," I said. "So far as I know, he hadn't tried to see Marty or anything."

Changing tactics again, Cabot skipped to a new question. "Did you see your father when you brought your stuff over Saturday morning?"

"Of course. He helped me unload the car."

"Was he dressed and ready?"

"I let them know I was coming by pretty early, so yeah. I'm not sure what time Aunt Daisy called to tell them when she heard about Marty. I know they didn't know when I got here. I learned about Marty's death from Officer Wilcox." I didn't like this line of questioning, and that more than anything else threw cold water on any interest I might have had in Detective Cabot.

"Thank you for your time. We'll be talking again," he said. "I heard you'll be moving back to the carriage house and that you were by the house today."

"I was. Mr. Spencer told me I could go by. I wanted to see if there was anything of Marty's there that I might want to make sure Aunt Daisy had." I hated lying and wished I'd thought to at least do that while I was there so I could verify I had. "And I wanted to see the place again. Morgan said he'd get the carriage house ready for me even though I didn't know if I'd be able to use it at the time."

"When will you be moving back there?"

"Tomorrow. I still have some laundry to do here and I want to take the day to get things set up, not just a few hours in the evening. I was planning to call a friend to move books and stuff back this weekend. My dad isn't a young man any longer and he's not interested in bringing all those boxes right back up out of the basement."

Cabot nodded and made notes and then looked at me. "Do keep us informed of where we can find you."

With that he turned and left. So much for sexy and interesting.

Chapter 21

The next day, after I heard my dad leaving, I started packing my stuff. I called my mom to let her know what was going on, so if she came home and found me gone, she wouldn't wonder.

"Let me help," she said. "I'm making Daisy some breakfast and then I'll be home to change clothes and shower. I can do your laundry before you leave."

She made it sound like doing laundry for me was a thrill. Of course, you never knew with my mom. One day it was great, the next, who knows?

"If I don't want to do it, it makes sense to take it over to the carriage house and Win can do it," I said. "I can't imagine that doing laundry is fun for you." It certainly wasn't for me, no matter how much laundry I did.

My mom chuckled a little and then sniffed. "I still want to see you. This whole mess is horrible. I heard a rumor that they're looking at your father now because I'm his only alibi for the time Marty was…" She couldn't even say it.

"I was there last night when we both got questioned. I was told to make sure the police know where I am."

"Which means they're so focused on us that a killer is walking loose. Landon came by yesterday when we got back from the funeral home. He paid his respects. He seems like a nice young man, but I can't believe they aren't looking at him. Marty dumped him."

"I thought he broke up with Marty," I said, trying to remember what Cheri said.

"Marty told us she dumped him, but maybe that was to save face. She was going through a lot then. We'd just learned that your Gram was terminal. You were coming home. Marty had had some trouble at work, too."

"What happened at work?" I tried to remember. I knew she'd mentioned something about another hygienist who appeared to be trying to steal her regular patients. The two didn't get along at all. If I remembered correctly, both of them had been talked to by the office manager and the owner of the practice.

"That woman, Darcy McClelland, was always

harping on about Marty not having good technique or something. You'd think she'd know better because Marty got honors in her class. Darcy was always complaining to Dr. Pitts about patients she saw that Marty had seen. Dr. Pitts spoke to Marty a few times. After that, he kind of realized that it was sort of an issue for Darcy and told her to knock it off, at least that's what Marty said." My mom sniffed again.

"I remember her talking about it. Didn't Dr. Pitts' chat resolve things?"

"I think so, but with everything else, you know. And Marty. She wasn't always easy going. She tended towards the dramatic."

That I knew very well. It's why I only sort of remembered what had gone on at her work. There was always someone who was making her life miserable and she didn't deserve it. I wonder if that was the reason Wilcox had talked her into challenging the will. Marty would have been put upon only getting a bequest even though she knew that's all that was happening. If Wilcox had tried to solve the issue by suggesting Marty do something, then Marty's lawsuit made sense. Wilcox wasn't some horrible person interfering, she was a friend trying to help.

Unfortunately, Marty had taken her literally and gotten us all into this mess.

Mom and I talked a bit longer and then I went

back to packing up my clothing. I'd wait for Mom to finish cooking for Aunt Daisy and then chat when she got back. It wasn't like I had big plans for the afternoon. Maybe I'd learn something about Marty's life if I talked to my mom. While I don't always get along with my mom, that doesn't mean Aunt Daisy didn't, and even Marty.

Given that Marty didn't have my psychic talent and need to use it, I had a feeling that Mom would have been happier if I'd been like my cousin, despite her own faults. After all, she'd stayed close to home and didn't do anything that might cause people to talk. What more could my mother ask for? I'm sure she'd have found something if I were like Marty, but still, sometimes it seemed like those were the only two important things.

I brought up a couple of boxes from the basement, some of the lighter ones. I could probably bring up one of the heavier ones, but I was saved from that by my mom coming in through the garage.

She came over and gave me a hug.

"When's the funeral?" I asked, realizing I didn't know.

"Tomorrow afternoon. Pastor Francis is going to announce it on the church's social media. Then we'll spread the word through friends, too. There'll be a big service at the church and it will be just family and close friends at the graveside." My mom started to break down a little when she said grave. No doubt she and Daisy had gone to the cemetery to pick out a place for Marty. I wondered how close she'd be to her father's grave, but I didn't ask. I'd find out tomorrow.

I hugged my mom. "You could have called."

"Pastor Francis was there," my mom said. "And it seemed like you had enough on your plate. At least Daisy and I don't seem to be suspects. I feel like everyone else I know is. Did you know that they questioned John Gardner for almost two hours the other day? They kept at him about how he knew Wilcox was there and why he thought you might be in danger. They even wanted to know if he'd brought any kind of weapon. All of those things should have been obvious when they got there and you and your father were out in the yard."

I hadn't known that and while I felt bad for Gardner, I was glad to know my dad and I weren't the only suspects.

"Well, you and Daisy have Pastor Francis. Morgan hasn't talked about being interviewed, so I don't think they suspect him."

"Morgan's lived around here forever. He wouldn't have had anything to gain or lose by Marty's challenge, so I think they let it go for now." Mom bit her lip, trying not to say more.

I knew what she was thinking. The fact that Morgan was black had probably had his named mentioned more than once even though there wasn't a shred of evidence that he could have done it. Still, a fair number of people who had lived in Seales all their life knew who he was. They knew he drove Gram's white Mercedes sedan very carefully about five miles under the speed limit wherever he went.

At one time, I knew, he hadn't always made sure to drive under the speed limit, but he was younger then and, he said, wilder.

"But then you kids came along and you were the apple of Miz Beauvoir's eye and there wasn't no way I was going to let you all come to any harm," he said. "I breezed through a stop sign once and nearly got hit and that was it. I was going to go slow and careful."

I had a feeling it wasn't just that we were the apple of Gram's eye that caused him to go slow. Morgan had doted on all of us.

Mom helped me pack up the car, taking the lighter suitcases and rolling them out there. I put some of the boxes in the back. I decided to go down and grab one of the heavier boxes of books from downstairs and bring it up to put in the back. She packed me some bottled water, just in case I didn't have any clean glasses in the carriage house—like that would happen.

“I’m only going across town.”

Mom was crying as she stood beside the car, putting things in it.

“I know.” She wiped tears from the corner of her eye. “It’s just that it reminds of when you went off to acupuncture school and I didn’t hardly see you at all for years. What if this had happened to you all the way out there? I can’t get over it.”

Then we were hugging again. My mom is normally the strong one between her and Daisy, but she wasn’t being very strong this time.

“Why don’t you go call Bobbie and let him know when to come for the funeral,” I said. “I think Dad talked to him last night, and I know he said he’ll take off from work even if he has to take vacation.”

My brother would be a grounding influence on my mom. He and his wife, Abby, would keep her busy around the kitchen and keep her chatting away. Abby would start talking about the way my mom wanted to redo the kitchen and giving her ideas and help take her mind off of what was going on. Or so I hoped.

“Will he stay at Mom’s, do you think?” Mom asked. “It’s so strange he was just here and everything was so different…”

“I know,” I said, patting her arm.

I got in the car to drive over to the house. It was an uneventful drive and I promised myself I’d call Eric about helping me move this weekend when I got there. Pulling into the driveway, I saw an unfamiliar car around the side of the house. I pulled around it, looking back.

I got out and was wondering if I should go to the door and talk to Morgan, but he came out. Following him was Detective Cabot.

Chapter 22

"Just getting here?" Detective Cabot asked as I stood looking up at him and Morgan. Morgan just nodded at me. He didn't offer to help with the suitcases, but he knew I wouldn't let him carry anything real heavy.

"I am," I said. "Is there a problem?"

"I needed to check into Mr. Brown's whereabouts Saturday morning seeing he's part of your alibi in coming back here," Cabot said. "Just crossing I's and dotting T's."

I looked at Morgan, who gave nothing away.

Cabot stepped off the stoop and onto the driveway. As he got into the unmarked car, he gave me a half wave and backed out, the engine a long, low hiss.

"Are you okay?" I walked over to where Morgan stood, still not moving.

"I'll be fine." He tried to give me a smile, but it was pretty shaky.

"It's okay," I said. "Whatever you had to tell him, you told him and it will be okay."

"I'm not sure he was just here to find out about your alibi, Miz Ash," Morgan said. "I think he was wondering where Win was, and I didn't see her that morning. You know how she goes and sees her mama on Saturday. Her mama lives just a block from the apartments where Miz Martina lived."

"Ah," I said. "I wonder why he didn't want me to know he was asking about Win?"

Morgan shook his head.

We looked at each other, worries etched across both of our faces. "Ain't no way that girl coulda hurt a fly. I'm worried that if she gets arrested, things could go bad for her."

Win was an American citizen, but her roots were in Mexico. Given the political situation, I more than understood why Morgan was worried.

"We'll make sure she's okay. I'll use every penny of Gram's fortune if I have to to get her the best lawyer. I have a couple of names I got from Mr. Spencer in case I need a criminal lawyer, but I haven't called anyone yet. If Win needs someone, she can call."

"You think it will get that bad?" Morgan asked.

"No," I said. "But if it does, we'll be prepared, and you can set your mind at rest that if something bad happens, you'll know exactly who to call for help if they try to intimidate her."

I looked at my phone and read off Tara Tincher's name for him.

"Can she represent you both?"

"I don't see why not. Win and I aren't suing each other."

Morgan nodded and went inside. I knew he'd write the name down and then get on the computer that sat in an alcove in the kitchen to check into Tara's background. I wondered where Win was and if she was back at work, or if she was in her room, as upset as Morgan.

I considered going to check, but instead unloaded the back of my car. Finished with the lifting and moving, I started putting things away.

There was a small laundry room on the main floor of the cottage, and I threw my sheets in while I put away my clothing and personal items. The boxes of books could wait. When I'd done as much as I could, I called Eric to talk to him about helping move some boxes on the weekend.

"I heard Marty's funeral is tomorrow," he said after agreeing to help.

"It is. Will you be able to be there?" I asked.

"Of course. We all knew her and liked her, mostly. I mean she had her moments, but don't we all. Have you heard anything about who did it?"

"We haven't." I sighed, trying not to. "I wish they'd find who it was, but so far they've focused on me and our neighbor and now they're looking at Win."

"She's one of your Gram's helpers, isn't she?" Eric asked. I often forgot that although we'd been good friends in school, he wasn't one of those who were often invited out to Gram's.

"Yeah. She's younger and she's been here maybe six or seven years," I said. "I can't imagine that she'd do anything like that. It's horrible that they'd even look at her."

"Pretty girl? Dark hair? A little younger than us?" Eric pressed.

"You could say all that," I said.

"I saw her and Marty in the tavern and grill a few weeks back. They were leaning close together and Marty looked angry. The other girl, who might have been Win, didn't seem all that angry, but it's hard to say. I waved at Marty, and the woman she was with just glared. Even if she wasn't with Win, but I think she was because my sister knows her sister, it's someone to consider. Anyone having words with Marty…"

"Which might include half the town, the way

it's going," I interrupted. "I mean even Cheri had words with her not too long ago."

Eric laughed at the idea of Cheri killing Marty, but now I had to consider that maybe we didn't know Win as well as we thought. Of course, Eric's sighting was weeks ago, before Gram died or right around. Marty might have been drinking too much and Win was trying to get her to take a ride.

I sighed, hanging up the phone.

There were just so many people. Any of them could have had a reason to murder my cousin. Of course, there was an easy way for me to eliminate Win from my suspect list. She'd probably touched everything in the kitchen a million times. Those things should all pick up something.

I switched the wet sheets from the washer to the dryer and then set off to check out the kitchen in the big house.

Chapter 23

Win was humming when I went into the house. The tune was rather sad and I wondered if she was trying to cheer herself up or working through her agitation about being questioned by the police. She wasn't in the kitchen. I glanced around and saw her moving in the study, doing some light dusting.

"That you, Miz Ash?" she called.

"It's me," I said. "Just putting away some food my mom sent with me that I know I won't eat out in the carriage house."

I had my own refrigerator out there. I kept it stocked with quick eats, but for real meals I came into the big house, at least I did when Gram was alive. I wondered how that would feel now that she wasn't alive. Win and Morgan would cook for themselves, anyway, so maybe I could join them.

I pushed those decisions aside, thinking that if Aunt Daisy lived in the house she might have them cook for her. Then I could join all of them. Not that Morgan would likely eat with Daisy. He never ate with Gram, although sometimes she could persuade him to have a cup of coffee with her.

Morgan's sense of what was appropriate was the main reason I wasn't just planning on eating with them. No doubt he'd find an excuse to be somewhere else if I did that.

I touched Win's favorite set of potholders, which were hanging in the alcove by the big stove.

I felt joy in cooking, a freedom, accomplishment. I saw Win working with her mom to learn to make something on the stove. Excitement when it worked. Given her height to the stove, she was probably only eight or nine, but she already loved cooking. There was a hug from her mom. So much love.

"Can I help?" Win asked, touching my arm from behind. She'd been so silent, or so it seemed. Had she been beating drums, I might not have noticed her.

"Just lost in thought." I turned, smiling at her.

Win nodded.

"I heard Detective Cabot was here earlier, talking to you and Morgan," I said, hoping that this would open confidences.

Win shrugged. "I guess everyone has to be questioned." Win was second generation American. Her parents had immigrated here and found work. She'd been born in Kentucky. She spoke with a slight southern accent with a hint of Mexico in some of her words and phrasing. She was equally fluent in both English and Spanish, speaking whichever one was the preferred language of the people she was around.

"Was it about a rather heated discussion you had with Marty a few weeks ago?" I pressed.

Win sighed. "Everyone knows, huh? So everyone blames the Latina." She started to swear in Spanish. Believe me, I knew swearing. Having taken the language in high school, I was not fluent by any means, but kids always learned how to swear.

"I hope the police aren't blaming you, just following up on leads," I said. I hoped it was true.

Win just looked at me, and then she sighed. "I shouldn't get mad at you. You were the first one they took in. At least they just questioned me here."

I nodded. "What were you and Marty arguing about in the tavern? Maybe that subject could be a clue to who hurt her." I just couldn't say murder.

"She'd been drinking a lot," Win said. "She was talking to some guy, a big guy with dark hair and tattoos. He looked tough, like, you know? And he was buying her drinks. I pulled her aside and told her to come home with me. She didn't want to. I tried to get Claire Wilcox to help—she was there too, at the bar, but busy with another guy who was almost as tattooed as Marty's guy. Claire wasn't as drunk, though. I think she was sober but wasn't interested in interfering in Marty's love life."

Win took a breath and sighed. "I didn't manage to get her out of there. I finally left. It was getting late and I needed to be here in the morning. I guess Miz Martina was okay because she never talked about that night."

A man with a tattoo. Well didn't that just sound like the ultimate mystery clue. Tattoos weren't that uncommon around here. What was a little uncommon was that Win didn't describe him as the cashier at the coffee shop or something like that. Even if you didn't know someone, lots of people were familiar.

"He wasn't familiar to you?" I pressed.

Win shook her head. "Not on my side of town or around here," she said quietly. "He might have been out from Versailles or Lexington. I think there was some sort of special music that night, you know how they do once in a while?"

The tavern and grill often had bands come in, mostly local. Sometimes they got one from one of the surrounding towns, or even Lexington, and that drew people who knew that band. People from out of town then gave the tavern a nice boost in revenue. Of course, now my search for who had killed Marty might require I go into the city and search for a tattooed man. Like that was going to work out.

"Thanks for talking to me." I touched Win's shoulder. People sometimes gave off impressions to me as well, though I'm far better at items. Win just felt sad and a little scared. There was anger too, but I had a feeling it wasn't about this discussion. It might have been about being suspected for a murder she didn't commit. It could also have been a more general anger.

Win nodded. "Let me know if you need lunch or dinner. Morgan and I eat at about five-thirty. I know it's early, but Miz Beverly ate early and we really haven't changed."

"What did you have planned for dinner?" I asked.

"I was just making meatloaf. If you don't like that, I can make something else."

"That's fine," I said. "I'm not sure if you should count on me, but I'll try to be there. If I'm not, I'll have some for lunch tomorrow."

Win nodded as if that was the most normal

thing in the world, though I felt weird giving her instructions. Normally Gram would have done that. Once Gram had settled the issue, I would have eaten there, or not. There was a lot to get used to.

Chapter 24

I headed back to the carriage house and pulled sheets out of the dryer. I carefully carried them up the walnut wood staircase to my bedroom. The room was a pale green, so light that you could hardly even tell it was green. The walnut finished hardwood continued upstairs, though there was creamy tile in the bathroom, creating a nice contrast to the pale walls. The windows were wrapped in white wood and had pale green shades in each one. The rug on the floor was green and cream.

Gram had a green, pink, and cream comforter on the bed and I used that, though I brought my own sheets. Hers were good, but I had mine from home, so why not. The sheets were a darker green but blended nicely with everything else, and I liked that. The room smelled of citrus and lavender. Morgan had dusted in there earlier, or maybe Win had, given that he'd talked about not wanting to climb stairs.

Although he talked about being old and not getting around well, Morgan could do something when he really wanted to. I smiled thinking of him. He was a nice man and had been very good to us.

I finished making the bed before going back downstairs to the main room. I looked at the computer I had set on the small desk in the nook. The nook itself was basically an extended bay window. When I had moved in before Gram had died, Morgan and Jaci had moved the kitchen table out and put in a small desk. It was mine, but I'd purchased it for the space and figured that if Marty wanted it that badly, she could have it.

I set up my computer there so that I could look to my left and see out to the garden and the pasture beyond and to my right and see the main room. It was angled so I didn't see the kitchen straight on, though it was easy to keep an eye on things if I were cooking. It was a pleasant place to do computer work, though I'd have to pull the shades behind me, which I got up and did.

I thought I saw movement in the garden, but couldn't make out the person. I didn't worry about it too much. Gram had people who came to take care of the lawns. Morgan managed the people who did that and things wouldn't have paused just because Gram was dead.

I sat at the desk and looked at the computer. Making a face, I leaned my chin on my hand to think. My latest thread was the one about the tattooed man. Win hadn't exactly given me a great description, nor had Marty talked about anyone she was seeing or hoping to see. Maybe tomorrow there would be a man with tattoos at her funeral and I'd have an idea of who he was. I could talk to him then.

Penelope Blue appeared and leaped on the desk and sat looking at me, not blinking.

"Well?" I asked.

The cat opened her mouth like she was going to meow, but no sound came out.

"I don't know who killed Marty," I said. "I'm working on it."

Penelope Blue just stared at me as if there was something else I should be doing, but I couldn't think of what. A shadow fell across the windows and I looked up.

A man was running across the gardens. I couldn't see his face, just that he was wearing a plain blue baseball hat that could have been for UK. I didn't see the logo. He was in jeans and, oddly, a long-sleeved t-shirt.

I wasn't sure what was making him run. Then

I saw Jaci chasing after him. She wasn't any taller than my runner but she was fast.

I hurried to the door to look out and see what was going on. The runner never turned to look but put on a greater burst of speed. He didn't look like a runner, really, his body a little too heavy. I mentally filed away what I could about the man while Jaci glanced in my direction and continued on with her chase.

Just as it looked like she might be able to reach out and grab him, a horse screamed in the distance and Jaci turned towards the sound, heading that way, barely pausing a step. Without thinking, I set out after her.

Chapter 25

I was winded by the time I got to the barn. It's a long structure, two stories with three cupolas along the top. Gram had it painted cream with pale peach for trim and a brown roof on top. It was a pretty building and a little unusual. Peach isn't a real common color. Naturally the split rail fences were all black, though a few had faded to gray, probably because they'd been redone late summer last year and had faded more than the rest.

I jogged into the barn, trying to catch my breath. Jaci had a pitchfork and was tossing out a snake from a stall. The horse that had been screaming at it was being seen to by its owner. The snake didn't look big nor poisonous. I wondered if the horse's reaction had more to do with the owner than its own fear of the snake.

"How did that get in here?" I asked. Gram had groundskeepers that took care of the pastures. While you can't get rid of all snakes, to have one in the barn was unusual.

"Sometimes they get in," Jaci said. She wasn't nearly as winded as I was, and I realized I probably needed to work out more.

The horse's owner was making cooing noises with the horse, her head against his. The horse was a big bay, well-muscled through the hindquarters, and I wondered if he had been bred to race. That was most likely, although whether he ever raced was another matter. The owner looked as though this was a horse of the heart as she ran her hands down the side of his neck, keeping her face touching his.

"Who were you chasing?" I asked.

"Don't know. He didn't belong here, that's for sure. When I asked him what he was doing, he took off. He wasn't in the barn, more over towards the gardens and the carriage house. I happened to be out here doing a little work and spotted him."

"It's odd that the snake showed up just in time to distract you," I said.

"Think he's working with snakes?" Jaci laughed. She was easy going. "We get people who shouldn't be here from time to time. Sometimes they're lost, looking for a different barn, or looking for someone here who isn't around. Sometimes they're looking for a quiet place to rest because they're homeless. They're the ones who tend to run."

I nodded. I didn't quite believe Jaci's suggestions, though I didn't think she was lying to me. She was just making up reasons someone could have been in the barn.

"Are you alone today?"

"I am," she said, putting the fork away, having disposed of the snake. "Matt will come in tomorrow. He worked alone last weekend. Morgan told me you were moving back into the carriage house."

"I am. Slowly, though, you know?"

Jaci nodded. "I hate moving. I'm glad I have the apartment upstairs so I can keep an eye on the horses. Everything okay, Rachel?"

Rachel gave Jaci a nod and a wave as she moved out of the stall for a moment, reaching down to find the hoses that were coiled all around the place to help people when cleaning up after their horses.

I headed out of the barn. I was hot and sweaty and sticky, thanks to a run in the heat. Still, I hurried towards the carriage house, looking for signs of the trespasser. I looked at the ground but I didn't see any footprints. I kicked at the grass, trying to decide what to do next.

"What's going on?" Morgan called from the porch.

"Jaci was chasing a trespasser off. Then a horse saw a snake, which she took care of." I headed towards the big house, not caring that I probably stunk. Morgan had smelled me when I smelled worse.

"I thought I heard a commotion," Morgan said. "Awfully convenient for your runner to have a horse start in. Get a few garden snakes now and then. Most of our borders aren't bothered by them."

I realized what Morgan wasn't saying. Wasn't it interesting that a snake had appeared to scare a horse, or its owner, at just the perfect time for a runner to get away? Of course, that was a lucky set up. Even Jaci would have had trouble setting something like that up. Chances were, I was just trying to find trouble in coincidence.

I guess I could be forgiven for doing so, considering how much was going on.

Suddenly, I felt this overwhelming feeling of sadness come over me. I just wanted to be alone to cry. I don't know why it hit me so hard, standing there with Morgan. I guess the running and the heat and the fatigue had made me realize just how much had changed.

I hurried away into the carriage house where I broke down in tears.

Chapter 26

The next day I wanted to work on finding out who had killed Marty. However, it wasn't to be. I woke late, enjoying the size of the large bed and relaxing into it. I loved the feel of the mattresses almost as much as I had loved the ones I'd left behind in Washington. Of course, Gram had asked me what I'd gotten. She'd made sure to get a mattress that was exactly the same, though I think she said she couldn't get the exact brand, but one with the same specifications. If anything, it was a better mattress than the one I had had.

I took a long shower, knowing that I didn't have to worry about anyone needing to shower after me. The carriage house had its own hot water heater. I looked in the refrigerator, glad to see that Morgan had stocked me with some yogurt. There were even nuts in the cupboard, though they came with a note saying if I wanted a real breakfast to come by the big house.

I smiled. It was thoughtful of him. I was nervous and sad and didn't want to deal with anyone right away. I was burying my cousin later that day. If the movies were any indication, I was likely going to run into police officers and perhaps even the murderer.

I was in shorts and a t-shirt when my phone rang. My mom.

"Ash," she said. "I'm going to need you over at Daisy's. Bring whatever you're going to wear this afternoon and get over here. She's falling apart and I'm…" She couldn't finish, dissolving into tears.

"I'll be there," I said to air as my mom had already hung up.

I went upstairs to stare into my closet for a minute. I had a gray and black dress that I'd worn for Gram's funeral. I almost missed seeing it, probably because it held such unhappy memories for me. But that was what I grabbed, along with some black ballet flats that I'd picked up to go with the dress. I wouldn't have to wear nylons or tights with it. My ballet flats wouldn't make my feet hurt, at least not much.

I put the outfit in the car, got my purse and

phone and then drove off. I saw Morgan look out the side door. I waved at him.

It didn't take long to get to Aunt Daisy's. Mom answered the door. I hadn't even set foot inside when I heard my aunt sobbing from the back of the house.

"She's in the bedroom," my mom said. I walked back with Mom. I sat on the edge of Daisy's bed, rubbing her back. My aunt had her head buried in the pillow such that I wasn't sure how she could breathe, much less sob at the volume she was sobbing at. I looked at my mom, not sure what she wanted me to do.

"I need to shower and get my clothing for this afternoon," my mom whispered, as if her voice would interrupt Daisy's sobs. I had a feeling nothing was going to do that. "I'll be back in a few. I just couldn't leave her alone."

If my aunt understood what my mom said, she gave no indication, just punching at her pillow from time to time. Her room smelled stale, as if she'd been sick and locked in for a long time. It was unlike the rest of the house.

I rubbed her back, sitting with her until she calmed a bit and seemed to doze off. We said nothing. I sat there and she dozed. It gave me plenty of time to think, though, wondering who could have done this to Marty.

As if reading my thoughts, my aunt sat up.

"Who could have done this, Ash? Really? Why? Marty could be a pain, I know that better than anyone, but she was harmless."

"I don't know," I said. I did wonder if it had something to do with her contesting the will. Not from me, of course, but who else would have benefited from me getting the house instead of Marty? I had no idea what she'd planned to do once she got the house.

In a mystery there might be a would-be acupuncturist who didn't want me to set up my business in town, but that was silly. I didn't think Marty was going to do or not do anything different from what I was doing, except she'd have lived in the big house. I don't know what would have happened to me, really. If she'd have let me live in the carriage house at a rate I could afford, I'd have lived there. If not, I'd have found an apartment.

Who benefited? No matter what happened, I was staying.

But did everyone know that? I thought about it. Who would it matter to if I left or if I stayed? I wasn't that important to anyone but my immediate family, at least not that I knew of. I had sold everything back on the west coast and planned to stay here. A change in the will wouldn't have made a difference.

The biggest loser, if Marty had won her challenge, would have been Penelope Blue, but I couldn't see the ghost cat killing someone. And even if she could, would a cat kill because no one else could see her? And even if she could, it wasn't like Penelope Blue could touch anyone. I couldn't even touch her, though I could see her.

"I blame that Claire Wilcox. I don't know what she said to Marty or how she got her to do it, but I know she's the reason Marty contested that will. I don't like her one bit," Aunt Daisy sniffed.

I didn't remind her that Claire had been killed too, also murdered, and this time in front of my house.

"I know it wasn't you," Daisy said, hugging me to her. "I don't care what that LeAnn says or how she says it. You wouldn't have done that to my daughter."

"She was my cousin," I said. "We'd have worked something out no matter how the lawsuit went. It's not like I wanted the big house."

Daisy smiled and sniffed. "Your mom wouldn't want me to mention this—she hates any mention of it—but your grandmother was psychic. She could see ghosts. I swear she talked to that cat, Penelope Blue, all the time though she'd been dead how long? And I know sometimes she just knew things she ought'n. It scared your mom half to death, but I found it rather comforting. I often wonder why she didn't see this happening and make arrangements for it not to. Or maybe what she did was the best thing after all?"

I shook my head. I was about to confess that I had some of Gram's psychic abilities and to explain the limitations of them—we both could only see impressions of things that happened, not predict what would—when my mom banged through the door in the other room.

"I'm back!" she called.

"She's going to tell me I need to eat something," Daisy said quietly.

As if she had her own level of psychic ability, my mom came in the room, "You're up. Maybe we should get you some breakfast. It'll carry you through the service later on."

Daisy looked at me and we both laughed, though Daisy's laugh was more than a little shaky.

"What?" my mom asked, hands on her hips looking from one of us to the other.

Daisy shook her head. "I can't eat. I'll shower though. I probably stink to high heaven because I haven't in a couple of days. Heaven forbid those who want to mourn with me have to smell me."

Mom helped her up as if she were an invalid. Aunt Daisy let her. I slipped out of the room, wandering into the living room. I picked up a photo of Marty. It wasn't that old. She was on a cruise with Landon back when everyone thought things were serious.

It was framed in a wood frame that had the name of the cruise ship on it. The picture was of her and Landon with a large life preserver framing their faces. The life preserver also had the name of the ship and the name of the town they were in on it. It was corny but the two looked happy.

I opened myself to those memories. There was a lot of joy from Marty. I felt hope, too, but I couldn't tell if it was Marty or her mom who had hope. I felt something protective that might have been Landon. It was strong and sweet and I almost dropped the picture because I hadn't realized he'd handled the thing. For a moment I thought I was getting impressions from his photo. Then I realized they would have picked out the frame together.

There was sorrow, too, but that was later on and less than the joy. There was confusion, a change. A hurt and misunderstanding. I became overwhelmed with confusion. I saw Landon trying to ask questions but not getting good answers.

My head felt as if it was spinning. I didn't know which way was which and what I should do next. Confusion. Who was she? Who was Marty? Why was she being like that?

I felt a hand on my shoulder and I let go of the picture. I hadn't picked it up, just touched. My mom was standing there, looking concerned.

"Sorry. Just lost in thought," I tried to smile

but knew I failed miserably. Landon had been confused, I think. Or maybe Marty. I had gotten so much about confusion that I wasn't sure what was what.

"It was definitely a picture of happier times," my mom said, running her finger along the side of the frame. She sighed.

To me that was a sign that she wanted to say something but wasn't sure how it was going to be taken. I waited.

"I miss her so much. But in the last months, probably shortly before you got here, she started changing, closing herself off from us. Sometimes I thought I didn't know who she was. And then that lawsuit..." Mom shook her head, as if that would clear some confusion. I wondered if that was the same kind of thing Landon had felt.

"I feel badly that I was blaming Claire Wilcox for all of that. I didn't know they were close. When I heard they were friends and then some of the stories, I thought maybe Claire had influenced her and brought her to a bad end. Now, Claire is gone too. And drugs...I can't believe..."

"I can't either," I jumped in. Mom was really reiterating a lot of the conclusions I had come to.

"Someone had to have done that to her. Not Claire, although for a while I thought maybe she had." Mom sniffed and blew her nose. In the background I heard the shower running. Daisy was cleaning up.

"It couldn't have been someone who knew her well because they'd have known Marty didn't use. She used to speak out about them pretty seriously." I moved to sit on the sofa.

"I'm sure they thought that we'd all think that those who speak out the most forcefully secretly have a problem with them."

"Clearly whoever killed her did something else that made the police think it was murder. They wouldn't have just listened to us."

"The syringe that injected her with the overdose wasn't there," Mom said. "It wasn't on the floor, it wasn't anywhere around. Someone took it."

I hadn't known that. I hadn't been asking questions except of Cheri and my father, and neither of them had shared that. Cheri knew general stuff, but not specifics. My dad probably hadn't thought to ask. Aunt Daisy would have. Aunt Daisy would have wondered if she'd missed something in her daughter's life. She'd have demanded they tell her why they thought it wasn't an overdose, if only for her own peace of mind. She'd have wanted to know she really hadn't missed something. They'd have told her there wasn't a syringe.

Someone had tried to make it look like a crime

but had gotten scared. It didn't seem like a smart criminal, unless they hoped to plant a syringe in my rooms or with someone else. That meant that perhaps Marty wasn't really the target. Someone else was.

Chapter 27

My dad came and drove all of us to the Raynor's Funeral Home in downtown. It's around the corner from the main street in an old antebellum style home set back from the side road. The sign is tastefully small and beige with brown lettering, so you have to look for it.

The white columns risc up from the ground and reach all three stories. I've only ever been on the first floor where the visitation rooms are. An elevator goes to the upper levels, which are used mostly for storage and for some office paperwork.

Light hardwood floors line the entry. There are two large rooms off to the left where viewings take place. A white desk, or perhaps more accurately, a counter, sits directly in front, where a hallway would once have gone before the building was remodeled. There were signs on the desk pointing to room one and another large sign standing next to the door of room one that had Marty's name on it.

The wall between the two visitation rooms was open so we had use of the whole thing. Marty's casket was cream. A spray of pink roses lay on the top of the lower half. Pink floral arrangements and yellow floral arrangements surrounded the casket. I had sent mom money to get an arrangement for me, and it sat on an easel with the words "cousin" on it. The smell of the white lilies in two shoulder-height urns overwhelmed all the other floral smells. I wondered who had sent them, or if Daisy had picked them out. They didn't match the other flowers. Maybe the funeral home kept them.

My brother and his wife were already there, looking uncomfortable as the only people in the room with the casket. They'd clearly gotten up early to make the drive and had come straight to the funeral home. There were plenty of folding chairs in the room surrounding the ones they sat on. It was going to be a big crowd.

Jonah Raynor held Aunt Daisy's hand as he led her up to the front.

The rest of us all hurried to Bobbie and Abby to give them hugs and greet them.

"Thanks for coming," Mom said. Like Bobbie would have missed this.

Abby pressed hands but didn't respond.

I sniffed. I ought to go look at Marty. That's what you do. I hadn't had a hard time looking at Gram, saying goodbye one last time. Marty was different. Maybe it was because she wasn't much older than I was. I sniffed.

We all stood around talking, clearly a relief to Bobbie and Abby who hadn't felt comfortable in the room before. Daisy was taking her time up front.

Pastor Francis arrived next. After pressing our hands and shoulders, giving my mom a hug, he went up to the front to talk to Daisy.

"I can't believe it," Bobbie said. "I mean Marty could be a royal pain, but I can't believe someone would kill her."

We all nodded, agreeing. Nothing new to be said, not really.

Mom regaled them with tales of what she knew about things, stopping when more people arrived, friends and loved ones.

Memories were shared, as such things are at funerals. We'd gone on well into the night with Gram's funeral. There were a lot of memories of her. There were fewer of Marty and very few that I didn't already know. I had learned things about my grandmother at her funeral, stories that hadn't ever made it to me as a child about her younger days. That had been enjoyable.

I shared my own Marty stories with a number of people. Many of them hugged me and said they knew I couldn't have done it.

LeAnn showed up with two other women, all dressed in dark black, practically wearing veils, which was ridiculous. It wasn't like she was a friend of Marty's. In fact, she was barely a friend of Daisy's.

My aunt had taken a seat near the front. Pastor Francis stood guard across the aisle of folding chairs as people greeted her. Mom went and sat with her, particularly when she noticed LeAnn come in.

LeAnn glared at me, a look that practically screamed that she thought I didn't have any right to be there. I wanted to scream that I had more right than she did but didn't give her the satisfaction of starting something.

Cheri arrived and joined Bobbie and me and my dad. Landon slipped in and tried to stay to himself, but Daisy grabbed him for a hug and tears. He seemed really broken up.

The room got crowded. Nearly everyone I knew was there, from Eric and his family to Win and Morgan. Jaci was dressed in nice black jeans. Cheri's family was there and they joined us. Even my ex, Rick, was there, dressed in black slacks and a tasteful white shirt with narrow gray stripes.

Win and Morgan joined my family and we chatted about our memories of Marty.

"She loved those horses," Jaci said. "She needed to work more with them. I don't know why she wasn't a vet tech or something rather than a dental hygienist. She could have run the barn if she'd wanted to."

"Money," Bobbie said.

"Like Ms. Beverly wouldn't have paid her well?" Jaci asked. She was looking at him with her head turned a little, hand on her hip. She was right. Gram would have paid Marty very well to run the barn, with or without a vet tech degree. She didn't have to work at a dentist's, but she'd made that choice.

I thought back to all the talks we'd had when I was leaving.

"I envy you going off and finding something without the family helping," Marty had said before I left for acupuncture school.

There were other times when she'd said I was lucky not to live around here. Everyone cared when I came home because I wasn't around all the time. She kept talking about maybe finding work somewhere else, but she'd never get paid enough to cover the costs of moving and then setting up on her own. Plus, she wouldn't have had a horse. I wondered how much her horse, Blackjax, kept her from leaving.

It all reminded me that yes, Marty had wanted to leave Seales and go out on her own, to prove herself. What had she been into when trying to prove herself?

"Miz Marty just wanted to be taken for who she was," Morgan said quietly. "I think she saw the house and the businesses as Miz Beauvoir's provenance and healing as Miz Ash's. She needed her own space, which was at the dental office."

Win nodded with him.

Bobbie shrugged. He'd gone off and been successful. He probably hadn't heard about Marty wishing to go away. Both he and I had left, but she hadn't. Maybe it was the loss of her father earlier on or maybe it was just that she didn't believe she could survive without Gram, the way she'd been forced to survive without her father.

As we talked, the time ticked by and pretty soon, the viewing part of the day was over and the service was about to begin. We quickly settled ourselves into the folding chairs, my parents, Bobbie, Abby, and I in the front row with Aunt Daisy.

Cheri and her family sat a few rows back. I noticed that Win and Morgan sat with Win's family towards the back, near Detective Cabot who was dressed in a dark suit and tie. He could just as easily have been working for the FBI as attending a funeral in that outfit.

He made eye contact with me and nodded. I wondered if that nod was supposed to be a quiet murmur of sympathy or a warning that he was watching me.

Chapter 28

The funeral itself was short. After, those of us who were going out to the graveside drove to the cemetery. Naturally everyone at the funeral wanted to know if there was a wake afterwards. Mom informed everyone it would be at the big house. This was news to me, and I was surprised that Morgan and Win hadn't said anything. Of course, with everything up in the air about whether I was the new owner or if it would go to Marty, perhaps they hadn't felt a need to share. Or perhaps they'd been told I didn't need to know. Detective Cabot came to mind for that suggestion.

The detective had stayed towards the side of the lobby, watching exiting funeral goers, some of them leaving to head to the big house to help the caterers who had no doubt been hired. Others would go home and perhaps fortify themselves before coming by later in the evening. I had no illusions that anyone would just stay home. They'd all come, if only to gossip.

The graveyard was just outside downtown Seales, up a slight hill that probably hadn't been good for too much else. There were plenty of trees lining the lower part of the hillside. Other trees, smaller ones like dogwoods and crepe myrtles, were placed strategically up around the graves.

At the top of the hill was a low brick building, like a ranch house, and beside it a taller brick building. The latter housed the above-ground burial spots, the former the offices for arrangements. I'd gone there with Mom and Aunt Daisy when Gram had died. Although she'd pre-planned most things, there were still papers to sign and we had had to plan the date and time.

It was a small group of us in the cemetery, all gathered under a blue tent that shielded us from the sun, the smell of freshly cut grass fighting with the musky scent of earth. The funeral home had brought the flowers with them and set them around while the rest of us had been saying goodbye to those who would just meet us again in an hour or so at the house.

This part of the service was also mercifully

short. In the late afternoon, it was hot and the sun beat down on my head whenever I had stepped outside the small tent that didn't have nearly enough space for all of us as well as the casket. After throwing in our handfuls of dirt, and in Landon's case, a red rose, most of us returned to our cars to head back to the big house.

I had ridden over with my dad, but Bobbie and Abby gave me a ride to Aunt Daisy's where I could pick up my car. My dad was staying with my mom, Aunt Daisy, and Pastor Francis to watch them finish filling in the grave. I had no desire to do that.

I pondered the fact that Landon had shown up. I had wondered about a spray of red roses that had sat next to my floral arrangement. No banner indicated that she was beloved or who it was from. I suspected Landon sent that one. The gesture made me want to chat with him at the wake to find out what he knew. After all, as the ex-boyfriend, he would certainly have been under suspicion.

At Gram's, I had to weave my way carefully up the long drive as there were already plenty of cars parked there. Fortunately, there was a bit of space just outside my carriage house. I noticed that Morgan had parked Gram's car near there rather than pulling it into the garage, probably to make sure I had some space to park my car and wasn't stuck parking on the street.

Behind Morgan's car was a van. Lettering on the side indicated it was a catering truck. I hoped that anyone else who worked there wasn't parked in the drive. We needed the space for people visiting.

Stepping out of my car, I heard voices coming from around the corner. No doubt the large French doors were opened onto the patio. Soft classical music played in the background. I walked around that way to see who was there.

Cheri was there with her mom talking to a woman in a dark caterer's uniform. Clearly they'd come here to help out. Cheri's mom would have had a quick word with Morgan about who needed to do what. Most likely that was why Cheri had hurried out right after the funeral, giving me only one quick hug and a wave.

"Ash!" Cheri said, coming over to me.

She gave me a long hug and then stood back. "How are you holding up?"

"Doing okay," I said.

"I saw that detective at the service." She waited for me to say something.

I only nodded. "I was surprised that Landon came to the cemetery with us."

"I'm sure Daisy invited him. She really liked

him. I think everyone was disappointed when he broke up with Marty." Cheri nodded her head.

"Ash," Mrs. Price said, coming over to me. She had a fancy paper cup with some sort of punch. With the French doors all open, our small kitchen table had been moved next to the opening. Another longer table had been placed where our kitchen table normally sat. It held various types of finger foods and punch. Nearby was a cooler of sodas and then pitchers of sweet tea and iced water. The island held more food and some flowers. Someone had blown up candid shots of Marty as well as her high school graduation photo and placed them on easels scattered around the great room.

I let Cheri's mom give me a hug while we chatted about all the stuff that people chat about at a funeral.

"I saw that nice detective at the funeral. Did he go to the cemetery too?" Stacy Price asked. I wondered if there was irony behind her comment about him being a nice detective or if she was just making conversation.

"He was at the cemetery as well," I said. He'd been back by one of the trees, out of the way, but in position to see everyone visiting. If there were mysterious people in dark coats and umbrellas watching us, he'd have noticed them.

"I think he's a nice man," Mrs. Price said,

looking me up and down. "Just the sort that you could settle down with."

"Mama!" Cheri said, clearly embarrassed that her mom was match making at a funeral.

"I'm just saying."

"He nearly arrested her!"

I didn't correct Cheri that it wasn't nearly arrested. She was shaking her head when Rick Darlington came over to join us. At that point everyone went just a little silent, wondering how I'd react to him being there.

"Rick," I said quietly. I hoped that someone would come rescue me with something to do.

"Hello, Rick." Cheri's voice about as cold as I've ever heard it. Certainly whatever went on with her and Rick hadn't ended any better than things with me.

"I'm real sorry about Marty," Rick said. "She was nice."

I nodded at him.

"I'm here if you want to talk," Rick said. "We all go way back."

"I'm here too," Eric said, coming up behind me and wrapping an arm around my waist. "And we go back almost as far, don't we? And if not, at least we don't have a messy breakup."

I wanted to laugh at Eric but loved how he was rescuing me, although it wasn't at all what I had expected.

"I'm sure Ash and I can work through things together, if Eric isn't enough help," Cheri added, joining in the gang up on Rick.

Rick looked from one to the other of us as if he didn't quite know what to say.

Mrs. Price took pity on him and pulled him over. "I heard you were doing real good at your job out there at the gas station. Whatever made you decide to apply? It's just not where I would have seen you, but it's so good to hear when our young men make something of themselves."

Cheri, Eric, and I waited until Stacy Price had pulled Rick away from our group.

"I'm not sure a gas station is making something of himself," Cheri muttered. "But thank heavens my mom pulled him away. I love you and all, but I spent way more time than I wanted to listening to him bemoan how you broke up with him. I swear he never got over you."

I rolled my eyes. "Ancient history. I thought he dated a bunch of folks after me. I mean Claire, Marty, you."

Eric laughed and pulled Chelsea over. His wife had been talking to Morgan and was just heading over. She carried a plastic cup with the punch.

"Only twice, and only because I needed to feel pretty again. Was that a mistake," Cheri said.

We all talked about things that had happened and how the service had gone.

"Daisy looked pale at the service," Chelsea observed. "Not that I expect her to look her best, but she looks almost as if she could be sick. I hope she's eating and getting some rest. Has she seen a doctor?"

"My mom is there," I said. "She's making sure Daisy eats or she's trying to."

A thought occurred to me. Chelsea worked at the school district, which meant she came into contact with a lot of people about our age who had kids. She could easily have picked up some gossip. She wasn't one to share, at least not with me too much, but she might answer if asked outright.

"I heard something about that detective investigating, Cabot," I said, "knowing Marty already. Did they actually know each other, or did he just know Marty because he worked with Claire Wilcox and those two were friends?"

Chelsea thought about it. "I hadn't heard, really. I mean everyone knew Marty, at least everyone who lived here for any amount of time. There was a time when she was getting to know Claire really well that they hung out in the tavern all the time. I know Bernice, who works in the tavern, says that Cabot shows up there fairly regularly."

So he could have met her. Could have known

her a little. No doubt he knew about her friendship with Officer Wilcox.

I nodded, turning over the information in my head. "It's just so strange after being in Portland to think of how everyone always knows everyone else around here."

Eric gave me a long look. It wasn't like I hadn't been gone to Lexington, which might not be big by the standards of Portland, Oregon—not that Portland was large by the standards of Chicago or New York—but Lexington was large enough that you didn't know everyone. He knew I was thinking something else.

"It's kind of scary that Officer Wilcox died, too." I said, hoping to hold off Eric or Cheri starting to press me on where I'd heard about Marty and Cabot. Cheri might think I was just wondering for an investigation, however, after her mom's comment, she might start thinking I was interested in something else.

"Oh, I know," Chelsea said quickly, as if happy to rescue me. Maybe she knew something I didn't and wasn't saying. If she did, Eric seemed unaware of it. "Imagine someone that would kill a police officer in a town like this."

We talked about that for a bit, but no one had any insights into Officer Wilcox's death, at least nothing new.

"I feel so badly for you," Chelsea continued,

"what with losing your Gram and then your cousin and having to find Wilcox's body. That must have been such a shock."

I accepted her sympathy for what it was.

Voices quieted for a moment and I looked around. Daisy had just arrived with my mom and dad. And with them, helping Daisy into the house, was Detective Cabot. He did not look happy.

Chapter 29

Conversations quieted as everyone watched Daisy come in. Mom looked worried as she followed in behind my aunt. Morgan immediately went over to help Detective Cabot. He gestured to the Detective's jacket, in case Cabot wanted to take off his suit coat, which had probably kept him uncomfortably warm throughout the afternoon.

I wound my way through the groups of people chatting to my folks, surprised at how many people had arrived at the big house, so many of whom I didn't know. But that's the way of funerals, isn't it? People you hardly know show up and remind you that you didn't know the person as well as you thought you did.

"What is it?" I asked when I reached my mom. She was standing next to the island.

"It was awful," Mom said quietly. She looked near tears.

"What?" My heart started to pound. Had someone tried to hurt Daisy?

My mom shook her head not saying anything.

"Mom?"

There was a sigh. My dad looked at me and hung his head.

This bothered me.

"Is Daisy okay?" I asked.

"It wasn't Daisy," my mom said.

I waited, getting frustrated.

"It was LeAnn. She and a bunch of her friends all gathered at the cemetery and surrounded Detective Cabot—he was standing a little ways from the graveside—and started loudly talking about how he needed to be following you because everyone knew you'd killed both Marty and Claire. At first we ignored it, but then Daisy went off on LeAnn. LeAnn got very heated. Detective Cabot ended up calling in another officer to disperse the women."

My heart hammered. Why would LeAnn start insisting that it was me? What was it that she thought she knew?

"But I didn't do anything," I said.

My mom patted my arm. "We know. That's

exactly what Daisy told them, but LeAnn has decided that since Officer Wilcox died after investigating you, then you must have done it."

I felt someone behind me and I turned.

Rick was standing so close that I felt his warmth against my back. At one time in my life that would have been comfortable. Now it wasn't.

"That's horrible," Rick said. He sounded almost happy about the fact that I was in trouble, or maybe he just liked the drama.

"Isn't it?" my mom said.

I moved closer to my dad, who put an arm around me, protecting me from having to stand too close to Rick. There was no Mrs. Price to rescue me from my ex this time, nor even an Eric. Too bad.

"I can't believe anyone would think Ash did it. It's so wrong!" Now Rick was building himself up as if he was going to go out and shout that I'd done nothing from the rooftops. As if he could be my rescuer or something.

Cabot joined us, slipping quietly into the group. He gave Rick a long look. "We don't need anyone else going off around here about who did or did not do anything. It's up to the police to follow the forensic evidence, and we'll be doing that."

"It's hard to believe my mom is such a good

friend of that LeAnn's," Rick said. "I'm kind of embarrassed."

Suddenly this was all about Rick and how things looked. It was just like him. I wanted to leave.

"You can tell your mom that I and the rest of the force are looking at everyone involved quite carefully. Officer Wilcox was one of ours," Cabot said.

Rick nodded. He gave me a long, puppy-dog look, which I did my best to avoid. What had I ever seen in him?

I wanted to talk about what was going on and say something, but I didn't want to have to engage Rick. I looked over at Cheri, who was talking with Eric and Chelsea. Abigail Burns had arrived and was over talking to Mrs. Price. Win chatted for a moment with Eric and started talking to the caterers.

"Miz Ash," Morgan said breaking in, "I'd love to get your opinion on something I'm working on, if this isn't a bad time?"

Rick opened his mouth.

"It's fine," I said. No one else interrupted me. My mom even closed up the hole that was left in the circle when I went off with Morgan.

"Thanks for the rescue," I said quietly.

Morgan chuckled and led me into the study. Hellspark and Babs were both on the window seat grooming each other. Penelope Blue wasn't around.

"I was wondering if you wanted to me to keep the study this way or if you'll want me to box up the housekeeping records Miz Beverly keeps in here and bring them over to the carriage house so you can review them? Or do you just want me to start delivering them to you?" Morgan asked.

"Can you just email them to me?" I asked. I heard the door open again. Morgan stuck his head out. One of the caterers was there, and they were answering the main door when the bell rang.

"I can do that," Morgan said. "But I'd advise going back about a year. I'll send those records, too."

"Why a year?" I asked.

"It'll familiarize you with the way things are being done now. It might also help to know what money comes in and what goes out, as well as helping you understand where the investments are. Your Gram owned a number of rental properties around Kentucky as well as being the majority stockholder in the bourbon business, you know. That's all yours now. It's not just a big fat lump of cash. It has to be managed."

I nodded. Something else I was going to have to do. Of course, Bobbie was in banking and Eric was an accountant, so I had friends who could advise me if I didn't like Gram's accountant. That was another name I had to come up with. So many details. In a way, Marty had saved me from having to be overwhelmed with that stuff when Gram died. Now I was going to have to find all of that out. No doubt there'd be inheritance taxes and what have you.

"This is starting to feel like so much. Gram had an accountant, didn't she? Someone to take care of that?"

"I did most of it," Morgan said. "She looked things over, but I did the advising. I can do that for you, but I'd recommend that we sit down with someone first. I just make sure bills are paid and income is routed to the proper accounts. The business has its own accountants, and we just get papers. The same is true for the rentals. We have someone who does the barn payroll and takes care of our taxes. We have a general accountant who does taxes. I'll send you the name of the person who takes care of the barn and our personal finances."

I nodded, thanking him.

We both slipped out of the study. I was glad to see Rick off talking to some people I didn't know. I wasn't up to dealing with him.

Cheri waved and walked over to me.

"Thank heavens," she said. "I heard what happened at the graveside. I cannot believe LeAnn."

"It's one thing to think I did it, but why would she want to upset my aunt like that?"

Cheri shook her head. "My mama might get something out of her later. I know I won't get anything because I'm your friend. Mama is just far enough removed, don't you think?"

Bobbie and Abby also wandered over, and we spent some time talking about everything that happened.

"Where are you staying?" I asked him. "You know you're still welcome here."

Bobbie and Abby had stayed at the house when Gram died. He hadn't talked to me about staying the house this time.

"I wasn't sure where things were with Marty's challenge, so I booked a hotel room. I'm only here for tonight. We'll drive back tomorrow," he said.

"I wish you had called. The house could have been used. Just not by me," I said.

"Yeah, but I figured this way if the challenge was still in effect, they couldn't argue that I took something." Bobbie gave me a smile.

"Are you going to redo that kitchen?" Abby asked.

I could see the ideas whipping through her head.

"At some point. First I need to sort through everything here and get things straightened out.

I'll be living in the carriage house. This place is way too big."

Abby looked a bit disappointed, but that didn't stop her from chatting about the house.

We wandered into the main room. My mom was sitting with Daisy on the sofa, my dad hovering around, trying to act useful. Mrs. Price was in the corner talking to Pastor Francis.

I noticed that my friend Thad was over in a corner talking to some people I didn't know. I waved at him and went over.

"Look at you," Thad said quietly. "I haven't seen you hardly at all and when I do, it seems to be funeral related. Can't you find a better reason to get together?"

"We'll have to do lunch or something," I said. "And you'll help me plan my open house when I get my acupuncture business going?"

"I wouldn't miss it," Thad told me, smiling a little.

Thad had studied business and ended up as an enrichment advisor to one of the aerospace companies north of Lexington. That meant he was always designing those events that were supposed to help employees bond. As I told him, he was basically a glorified event coordinator.

Landon walked over and Thad went silent, looking down.

"Ash," he said. "I am so sorry about Marty."

"Thanks," I told him.

"I'm sorry about everything that's going on with LeAnn. I think I may have contributed to her belief that you might have done it. When Marty was changing, I thought maybe it was because you were coming home. I thought Marty wanted to be someone who would impress you. Plus, I think LeAnn worries if you didn't do it, I might have." Landon still hadn't met my eyes.

"Why?" I asked.

"LeAnn is a cousin," Landon said.

Chapter 30

I still wasn't sure why LeAnn was so gung ho to pin the murder on me. Just because Landon was a cousin of hers didn't mean I had to kill Marty. I waited, watching Landon's face. In the background people milled about, talking softly. One of the caterers took out a hot plate of savory tarts that smelled like cheese and garlic. My stomach growled.

"I know," Landon said, shuffling his feet like a teenage boy.

"I don't," I said.

Thad was looking away, like he was trying to be invisible. I wondered what was up with the two of them. I didn't even know Thad knew Landon.

"It's just that I think LeAnn thought I'd been stupid to let Marty go. I was the one who broke it off. She was always on me about being foolish because your Gram had money. We're not rich, not like your family." Landon said that almost belligerently.

"Then Marty didn't get anything after all," I said. "Which meant LeAnn no longer had a reason to push you to get back together with Marty. She should have been pleased."

"That only made her more angry, like the universe was conspiring against her. Plus she liked Claire Wilcox. She didn't know her, not really, but Claire was nice to her when they did speak. I guess she met her at the tavern and grill when she worked there for a month or so. Claire always gave good tips. When she started saying she thought you had do it, LeAnn took that as gospel." Landon looked really upset.

"Besides, I think deep down she's certain I did it. She's actually my second cousin once removed so I don't know how related we are, but I've known her all my life. She knows I've been known to lose my temper and throw things."

"So if she believes I did it, she doesn't have to think you might have," I finished for him.

Landon nodded.

Thad was still silent but he moved slightly closer to me.

"I guess I just wanted to apologize and explain," Landon said.

"Thanks," I told him quietly.

I watched him walk off. Daisy called him over to her by the sofa, and he went over there. The women around my aunt made room for him and clucked over him. If anyone believed he had killed Marty, I didn't think they were in the room. He did seem like a nice enough guy. I hadn't gotten any impressions that there might be a problem.

"Don't trust him," Thad said.

"What's up with you two?" I whispered. "You about hid behind me."

Thad gave me a half grin. He's short and he's sweet and he dresses like the queen he is. He might have worn black for Marty's funeral, but he had on a dove gray shirt with a black and gray ascot that made the outfit look like he'd just come from a royal do rather than a funeral.

"When I first started out doing enrichment events, I did a few freelance things around town. I put on a party for this group of guys that Landon knows. They're all big UK fans and it needed to be a Wildcat theme. Who better to do it, right? I mean I went to UK as well. But everything I did was wrong. They wanted something new and different, but my ideas for new and different just weren't right. Landon was the worst of them. He'd let me go on and then say, 'Next!' like it was that easy to come up with a million ideas. They had no idea of the party they wanted. I finally quit the job, gave them back their deposit. They were still pissed, though, because they insisted I'd wasted their time and never intended to do anything."

"That's rough," I said.

"I was a lot more careful about who I called back on jobs after that. Birthday parties were much easier. It got me an in with a lot of places because they knew me, at least a little." Thad was looking around now, more his usual self.

"Do you think Landon even remembers?" I watched as Thad's eyes skimmed the room, remaining a bit longer on Detective Cabot than on others. If it was just admiration, I couldn't blame him. There was something about the detective. On the other hand, perhaps Thad and Cabot…?

Couldn't be. There'd definitely been some flirting with me. Wasn't there?

"Oh, he remembers," Thad said. "I ran into him with Marty once, and he said something to her. I never heard the end of it. I ended up leaving the restaurant because they were constantly on me. I was with a guy I'd just met, and it completely ruined our date."

I raised an eyebrow.

"It surprised me that Marty would be that mean. To be honest, I think even Landon was a bit embarrassed. I think he wanted to make a snarky comment and have it end at that. Marty was the one that wouldn't let it go. While he played along a little, towards the end, when I was planning to leave, I think he was trying to get her to shut up. Even the waiter was looking uncomfortable."

"I never would have expected that about Marty," I said.

"Neither would I," Thad confessed. "I don't know what got into her. She didn't seem drunk."

I bit my lip, thinking about it. It didn't sound like drugs. It just sounded like meanness. It wasn't that Marty couldn't be cruel, but mostly she was thoughtless in her cruelty. This felt deliberate, if Thad was relating the experience accurately. He could be a bit of a drama queen.

"Was anyone else around that you knew? Was she showing off for them? It sounds like it made Landon really uncomfortable too."

Thad shrugged. "I didn't see anyone, but I don't know that many people. I live in Lexington and try to stay there. It's big enough that I fit better."

I understood that. Thad had always had a hard time with people dealing with his sexuality. He was, in turns, outgoing and open about it, only to switch off and become very closed and private. What he didn't understand was that very changeability made it hard for people to relate to him, at least from my perspective.

"I've heard Marty had changed," I said. "I hadn't heard that anyone thought it had to do with me, though."

Thad shrugged. "I'm not in the gossip circle. For that you need Cheri." He gave me a smile and patted my arm.

I watched him go talk to Cheri and my brother, leaving me alone. I wandered over to where my mom sat. I didn't see Rick, but I didn't want to give him the opportunity to corner me and suggest that I needed his protection. The thought made me shudder.

"We need to chat," Detective Cabot said, coming up next to me. He nodded towards the front.

My heart hammered worried about what exactly he needed to chat about.

Chapter 31

Once again, I was back in the study. No one else was around. Hellspark and Babs took one look at us and decided to make for the upstairs. For cats living in the quiet environment of an older woman, they were generally quite social. However, they did like their own space and they didn't know Detective Cabot at all.

Penelope Blue hadn't shown herself to me, either, but then she only tended to do that when she thought whatever was going on was important. I was never quite certain how it might be important, but I tried to pay attention when she did show up.

"So what's up?" I asked. I wanted to cross my arms, but tried to avoid doing that so I didn't look defensive.

"I'm concerned about LeAnn VanderPlank and her friends," Cabot said. "She's gotten it into her head that you murdered your cousin and Officer Wilcox. She's willing to say anything to anyone. It might be time to consult an attorney about slander. She's been told on multiple occasions that we are pursuing multiple avenues of investigation, but at this point there's nothing that links you to the crimes."

"Thanks, I guess." I wasn't quite sure what to say. Wasn't it unethical for the police to warn me about someone like that? Or maybe it would be unethical not to? What if LeAnn took things further and someone tried to kill me?

Cabot nodded. "I know this is hard. Losing two family members so close together and then this situation." He reached out like he was going to touch my hand and then drew back.

"I'm sure you're in an awkward position, too," I confessed. "I guess you can't completely write me off as a suspect. I did have a reason—at least it would look like one to most people."

Cabot gave me a genuine smile, one that seemed to make his eyes twinkle. "You'd think being a police officer I'd be used to awkward situations, but they always seem to pop up. It's what I get for living in a small town."

"I'd like to say at least you don't get a lot of

murders, but that's not even true here." I gave him my own smile. Were we actually flirting?

The idea made my body go warm and fluttery. It wasn't great flirting from either of us but again, awkward.

"Are you okay in there?" Rick asked coming around the corner, eyeing Detective Cabot as if he were going to fight him.

"We're fine, thanks," I said, making no move to leave the study. I did not want to talk to Rick.

"That's good. I mean it's got to be awkward to be investigating the death of a woman who turned you down," Rick said walking into the study. He was actively glaring at Cabot.

I raised an eyebrow.

"I may have spent some time with Marty, but we were never anything more than acquaintances," Cabot said stiffly. "I talked to the captain about the relationship when she was initially found."

Relationship? I looked at him, raising an eyebrow, waiting. He'd been in the one vision I'd had, at least peripherally.

"When Marty became friendly with Officer Wilcox, she joined most of the officers and detectives at the bar from time to time. When Landon was working late, we had dinner together a couple of times." Cabot was definitely explaining to me. He wasn't even looking at Rick.

"Marty was friendly that way," I agreed. I filed that information away. Could I have two cops who would be after me? Was Cabot's friendliness just to get me to open up? Or could he possibly be trying to get into my home so he could plant the syringe? I mean, why would I take it from Marty's home, but seeing as it hadn't been found there, it could have been tossed away anywhere.

I'd have to go through the house, looking in the trash to make sure there was nothing there. I didn't need any more evidence pointing towards me. The warmth in my body chilled at my suspicions. I didn't want to believe he'd do that, but until I knew who had killed my cousin and Wilcox, I couldn't really trust anyone.

Cabot nodded at me.

"Thanks for letting me know about LeAnn," I said quietly when it looked like he was going to leave. I moved to follow him, but Rick put himself in my path.

"Excuse me," I said.

Rick made like he was going to grab my arm. Fortunately, Cabot turned and waited for me. It wasn't lost on me that he was noticing the way Rick was trying act as if he and I were a couple.

I avoided Rick and moved out into the entry.

"Thanks again," I whispered to Cabot, standing closer than perhaps I really needed to.

"Is he a problem for you?" Cabot asked, turning. Rick was following along but Cabot's voice had been low enough that he probably hadn't heard.

I shook my head. He was a problem, but it was my problem. I didn't need to involve the police with Rick. Or maybe I did.

I hurried back over to Cheri, who was talking to Jaci, of all people. Cheri is the most un-horsy person in the area. I had to wonder what she had in common with Gram's head groom.

Chapter 32

The wake wound down, finally, as these things do. Daisy tried to help with cleaning up, but Morgan made her sit that out while the caterers did their work. She was welcome to stay in the house, but she couldn't help clean up.

When everyone else was gone, my mom and dad took her home.

Bobbie and Abby had left about an hour before to go check into their hotel and have a real meal, he said.

"Call me if you want to change up that kitchen," Abby said. "I'm kind of far away to work on it with you, but I'd be heartbroken if you didn't at least let me help when you're shopping for ideas."

I hugged her and thanked her. I knew she was just dying to help out. That's what Abby did. I hoped that my mom would take her up on kitchen remodeling, at least. That way if I decided to keep Gram's kitchen as it was, I wouldn't hear about it all the time.

Cheri left only a little before my folks. Her mom had left earlier.

When it was just me and Morgan and Win, I slumped down on the sofa, not ready to go back to the carriage house. This had been harder than Gram's funeral.

"Do you need some dinner, Miz Ash?" Win asked.

"I'm good, thanks. Do we have leftovers from the wake?"

"We have plenty. If it's okay with you, I'd like to take some to my mama. She was here for a bit earlier on. She liked those little pinwheel sandwiches."

"Definitely take her some," I said. "You should go now. It's been a long day for all of us."

"Thank you, Miz Ash." Win nodded at me and moved to the kitchen where I heard her pulling the pinwheels out of the refrigerator and making a plate for her mom. She could have just sent some with her mom while she was there, but she was probably worried about how that looked.

Morgan was in the other room with the vacuum cleaner making sure the house was as spotless as he could get it.

I closed my eyes for a minute, breathing in. It was nice right then. I could pretend that Gram was upstairs and would be down any minute. I could even pretend it had been a family party, at least for that instant.

I felt the lightest chill on my thighs. My eyes snapped open, but I was unsurprised when it was Penelope Blue standing on me. She didn't often sit on me. Mostly she paraded around for me.

"What is it?" I asked her, knowing that Morgan would never hear me over the vacuum.

She opened her mouth like she was going to meow. The she leaped off my lap and ran over towards the kitchen. I stood up to follow her, feeling rather foolish. Maybe she was just repeating a routine she'd had with Gram, running to the kitchen to get fed. Gram might not have cooked for herself, generally, but she always fed the cats, right up until she couldn't get out of bed any longer.

Instead of going to the back corner of the breakfast nook where her food dish was, Penelope leaped onto the chair that was closest to the big bay window and made a point of looking out. If she were a ghost dog, she would have stood on point.

I came over and looked out. The lawn was filled with shadows. The crepe myrtle was moving slightly in a breeze. The other bushes, some laurels and burning bushes, were still, though that wasn't unusual. The flower beds seemed as if someone had stepped in them but they probably had. Morgan would have the groundskeepers take care of it when they came. I didn't think much of it.

No one ran through the yard like the guy the other day. No one suddenly popped up with a face at the window to scare me. I looked out, wondering what was bothering Penelope Blue.

I wandered back into the kitchen. I'd eaten some of the finger foods that we had ordered from the caterers so I wasn't hungry, not exactly, but I felt at odds. I'd been around people for so long that I wasn't quite decompressed from all the talking.

I turned to find that Penelope had disappeared. I walked over to the front and waved at Morgan so he'd know I was going home.

He turned off the vacuum. "You okay?"

"As good as I can be, I guess. How about you?"

Morgan nodded. "It's a hard thing to lose a young one like Miz Marty. Miz Beverly was ready to go, or at least as ready as she'd ever be, so she said. But Miz Marty. She was still young. Such a shock. And a murder." He shook his head over and over as he spoke.

"Yeah. Detective Cabot said that I should think about contacting a lawyer about slander given what LeAnn is saying."

"You going to do it?" he asked.

"I probably should. I'll call Nick Spencer in the morning." He hadn't been there today, though he and the office staff had come to Gram's funeral and the wake, at least briefly. Of course, no one at his office had known Marty. I didn't doubt that Mr. Erickson would have come if Gram were still alive, but I wasn't the client that Gram was. At the rate I was going, I might be that sort of client for the local criminal attorney.

"They always did a good job for Miz Beverly. I 'spect they'll do it for you, too. The Beauvoirs are a good family. All of you." Morgan nodded again as if that would make his point.

"Thanks, Morgan." I went over to him and gave him a hug. He seemed faintly surprised but hugged me back, a quick, tight thing. Then he moved back to his place by the vacuum. I turned and left through the side door.

The sun was low in the sky but it wasn't yet dark. The shadows were long and the breeze was pleasant. I didn't hurry. At my door, I looked towards the backyard once again, trying to see whatever it was that Penelope Blue had been trying to show me.

I saw nothing out of place, but I couldn't help feeling that I was missing something. That made me uneasy as I unlocked my door and entered the house.

Chapter 33

Tired, I went upstairs and decided to shower. I figured an early night would be just fine. Maybe I'd even read. Naturally, after showering, when I'd washed the smell of the graveside off, I was more energetic. I put on sweats to go downstairs and have a snack. Apparently a bit of relaxation, and suddenly my energy and my appetite came back.

There are always crackers and peanut butter in the cupboard, so I had a few of those while settling in on my computer. It was dark enough that I should have turned on a light, but I found the light on the computer was enough. For some reason, I sort of wanted to see outside. It was like an itch. Maybe it had been Penelope Blue running to the window to look out, I don't know.

When I looked up from the Facebook posts I was trying to lose myself in for the fifth time, I wondered why I was so interested in outside. I couldn't put my finger on it, but I almost felt like a heroine in a horror movie, staring down the hallway, waiting for the monster.

The windows rattled in a gust of wind.

I jumped.

I laughed at myself, just a little, but I was nervous. It would be nice to have a cat with me. I wondered how Hellspark and Babs would do in the cottage. They were used to far more space, but they really spent most of their time in Gram's study or upstairs. Of course, when Gram had been alive, they followed her everywhere. Those two rooms probably smelled the most like her.

There wasn't a shortage of cats in the shelters, and I could always adopt one and bring it to the cottage. It wouldn't help me that night, though.

For an immediate comfort, I could probably find a particularly friendly barn cat who would be willing to comfort me. The last thought was almost enough to get me to put on some shoes and go out hunting for a friendly feline.

Instead, I sat in the chair looking out, wondering what exactly I was looking for. The only thing that moved in the yard were the trees, sometimes the bushes.

My eyes got tired and I started to fidget. Still, I

couldn't pull myself away. I had no idea what I was waiting for.

I must have sat there an hour before Penelope Blue showed up, popping in as she often does, standing near my computer, looking out.

I refocused on the backyard, wondering if she was looking at something or if she wanted me to notice something.

A light came on in the far wing, the one where Win and Morgan had their rooms. It was too far down the hall to be Morgan, so probably Win. I hadn't heard a car but that didn't mean anything, not really. I wasn't listening for her.

Still, I watched the light. Another turned on and then both went off.

The wing was dark again.

Win and Morgan might be meeting in the main house, having a late evening snack. If I went over there, likely I'd find the two of them together talking about the wake. They'd let me join them. My stomach growled slightly and I figured what the heck.

Even Penelope Blue leaped down from the desk and waited by the door.

I put on a pair of shoes and headed over to the house.

I had to unlock the side door. Morgan had been busy in that sense, getting the house taken care of. I slipped into the big kitchen, expecting to see Win and him, but it was dark and silent.

I heard the vacuum upstairs now. I walked through the big room and up the wooden stairs, looking down.

I turned the corner to see Morgan running the vacuum in Marty's old room.

"Hi," I said.

He jumped seeing me. Then he turned off the machine.

"Miz Ash. Did you need something to eat? I can go whip you up something."

"No," I said. "I just saw the lights in Win's room go on and off and thought maybe the two of you were down in the kitchen. I figured you'd have been talking. I didn't realize you were still working."

"Win called earlier and she said she was spending some time at her mama's talking. Didn't expect to be back until later," Morgan said. "So if you saw a light on in that room, it wasn't Win."

I frowned. Morgan looked uncomfortable.

"Do you think someone is here?" I asked, almost a whisper.

"I wouldn't have heard anyone come in, but the doors are locked." Morgan said. He too whispered. Then he drew himself up and pushed the vacuum to a corner. He headed out and down the stairs.

"Do your rooms lock?" I asked.

"Of course," Morgan said, "that doesn't mean we use the locks. Just us and Miz Beverly. I used mine a bit when Win first moved in but decided it was foolish as Miz Beverly had far more interesting things to take than any of my old stuff. I think Win feels the same way."

I followed him through the house and down to the newer wing. The floors here changed to vinyl plank, something Gram had added just a few years ago when it started to get popular. You couldn't see it from the main rooms, and there was a door separating the areas. The vinyl was still nice looking and except for the feel, I'm not sure I would have noticed a difference.

There were rooms on either side. One had been set up like a gym for when Gram wanted to work out. There were mats on the floors and mirrors along one wall and a ballet bar. She had a treadmill in a corner and a bench with a few hand weights.

Morgan's room was across the way. He passed those rooms, a large suite with only the one door. I knew he had a small sitting area and living room and a nicely appointed bathroom, which Gram had decorated to his preferences, or as best she could. I remembered talking to her when she'd been doing it, saying getting Morgan's real desires out of him was probably harder than sending him to the dentist to have a tooth pulled.

The next door belong to Win. Her rooms were at the end of the hall, and across the way was a big open room with a pool table. I'd played down there several times. The room had windows all along the side and it was large enough that you didn't have to worry about hitting the glass with the pool cue.

Morgan knocked on Win's door. There was no answer.

We opened it and walked in.

Morgan flipped on a light. Her sitting area was a tidy area with a love seat in a bright pink and blue floral print along one side. A small television sat on an eight cube bookshelf across from her. She had a small electric fireplace sitting next to the door we'd entered, probably to offer ambiance. The window was directly across.

There was a hall near the entry. On one side was a compact area with shelves and a small refrigerator and microwave. The other side had the bathroom. Beyond it was the bedroom with a huge walk-in closet that was large enough to be a second bedroom.

Of course, anything that didn't fit in the rooms, Gram would certainly have made a space for in the main house. Given how long Morgan had been with her, she'd probably even have expanded his space, perhaps into Win's space and then making the room with the pool table over into Win's rooms.

We used it, but to Gram, the comfort of the people living there came first. As she'd gotten older, she didn't use the table nearly as much. Though most of the rest of us still got in a game or two, it wouldn't have hurt to not have a pool table around.

Nothing appeared out of place and Win wasn't around. On the dark-colored nightstand by her bed was an empty phone charger. Out in the front room, she had a second charger near the love seat and that, too, was empty.

Morgan frowned and pulled out his own cell phone and dialed Win.

I glanced around the place looking at her things, feeling guilty that I'd just entered her home. Of course, I had seen a light. Penelope Blue clearly thought it was important.

Morgan hung up the phone and shook his head. "She's still at her mama's, but now she's thinking she should come home just in case someone was here."

"We should call the police," I said. "There were a lot of people here. Maybe someone found a closet to hide in and stayed behind."

The idea clearly hadn't occurred to Morgan

and he looked shocked. His fingers shook a little as he dialed.

I worried I'd had a hallucination. If someone was going through Win's stuff, shouldn't something have been out of place? What did they want?

Chapter 34

It was late, so I shouldn't have been surprised or disappointed that Detective Cabot didn't come to the house. Instead it was a young, very blond man named Gil Daffney. Daffney was of average height and slender enough that his shirt seemed to bag around his middle.

He'd beaten Win to the house and was at the front when I saw her car cruising slowly up the driveway. She turned to look at us, shocked but then apparently pleased that we'd reached out to the police.

Morgan took Daffney around the house. I stayed downstairs, and when Win came in, we chatted.

"I can't imagine why anyone would have been in my rooms. If Morgan didn't say it was him, there shouldn't have been anyone," Win said.

"It's possible someone stayed behind from the party." She stood very close to me, as if by doing so, we'd be safer. I patted her arm.

"Morgan and I both looked to be sure everyone had left," Win protested. "We went through the whole house."

"Did you look in closets?" I asked.

Win shook her head, beginning to blush.

"There wasn't any reason to," I continued. "I mean, why would anyone try to hide to stay behind?"

Win nodded, realizing I wasn't blaming her.

"I bet you didn't check the attic either?"

"We'd probably have heard that. Those stairs squeal like a dying rabbit when you pull them down." Win tried to laugh a little at that, but her smile died just as quickly.

"Really?" I asked. "Morgan usually keeps up on that."

"When your Gram stopped needing to go up there, we didn't have much reason to go. I think we've been up about once every three months or so now. Morgan mentions he's going to oil them but he hasn't, at least not that I know of. Of course, if they went up earlier, when there were plenty of people here…"

Win let the last part trail off.

We were so busy talking to each other that no one would have heard a thing or if we had, there were so many other things going on, the noise would have been chalked up to the caterers or something.

I winced as I heard the squeal that Win was talking about. Clearly Daffney was being thorough.

The two of us waited down there, keeping an eye on the doors. Chances were if someone were fleeing from the police and Morgan, they'd have to go by us. Even if we didn't catch them, we'd see them. With two us, there was less of an issue of getting hurt.

Finally, the two men came back downstairs.

"I checked the all the rooms upstairs, the attic, the closets, the bathrooms. I didn't see anyone in the obvious hiding places, but this building is large enough that I can't guarantee that I didn't miss someone," Daffney said. "However, I'm reasonably certain no one is up there. If there is someone in the house, they're down here."

I waited.

"I'm going to leave Mr. Brown by the front door and have you two stay here. You'll be able to see or hear the side and back doors and the stairs. He can see the front rooms in case someone is in there," Daffney said.

We nodded. If Daffney were willing to leave us there to watch, as he said, he must have been fairly confident that no one else was in the house. It was certainly possible that whoever had been in Win's rooms had left when I went upstairs to talk to Morgan. The sound of the vacuum cleaner would have covered any sounds the intruder made.

Daffney started in the front and worked his way back. He checked the pantry and the coat closet. He looked in all the rooms and opened every door he found. I heard him open the door to the new wing and close it behind him.

We waited.

Daffney didn't take very long down there, but he did look puzzled when he came out. He was holding a baggie with something in it.

"What's that?" I asked as he got closer.

The baggie clearly held a used syringe. I hadn't noticed anything down that way when I'd been there with Morgan, but wc hadn't bccn searching the closets, just looking to see if anyone had messed with anything.

"Who has the rooms in the far back?" Daffney asked.

"Those are mine," Win said.

"Where I saw the lights go on when Win wasn't here," I added.

"This was in the coat closet in the front,"

Daffney said, holding it out. "On the floor. Is it yours?"

Win shook her head, looking puzzled.

"Are you aware that we're looking for the syringe that may have been the vehicle for the overdose of drugs given to Martina Beauvoir?" Daffney asked. Gone was the affable police officer now that he'd found something incriminating.

Win placed a hand over her heart.

"I'd never... I didn't..." she stammered, looking from Daffney to me.

"I'm sorry, ma'am, but I'm going to have to ask you to come to the station with me. We'll have further questions."

"What about the intruder?" I demanded. "I saw lights on here."

"I'm seeing no sign of anyone breaking in, however, we will be taking a further statement from you," Daffney told me. "Detective Cabot has been called."

With that, he led Win out the front door of the house. For questioning.

Chapter 35

Morgan and I weren't sure what to do. The house seemed quiet after Daffney took Win outside. I wandered around the kitchen, touching the tiles, the appliances.

Morgan seemed just as lost. He picked up a feather duster and was running it over the mantel above the fircplacc, ovcr and ovcr again. Hc continued to sigh.

Finally, I left the kitchen and went into the new wing. I walked into Win's rooms, not even thinking that I was violating her privacy. I knew she hadn't done anything. I touched the doorknob to her coat closet, hoping to get something.

Mostly I got Win, sometimes upset, frequently worried but mostly happy. I felt her though the knob. I saw coats going in and out of the closet, light jackets for spring and fall, heavier coats for winter. She worried about her mom, and her mom's face came up again and again for me.

There was a hint of something, a dark thread of anger and frustration that didn't seem to fit with the Win I knew. In fact, it was a jarring sense, but I had no idea who came with it. It was just an emotional feel that there was someone else who had touched the door, perhaps frequently or perhaps just once with a lot of emotion.

Morgan cleared his throat. He was standing next to me in the room. I started.

"You're like Miz Beverly, aren't you?" Morgan asked.

"What do you mean?" I removed my hand from the knob as quickly as I could.

"She'd touch things and she'd know things. Always could find when I misplaced something. She did for Win too, though Win don't know about it. Prob'ly scare her, being a good Catholic girl and all." Morgan gave me a smile.

I nodded. "I don't talk about it much."

Morgan nodded. "Must be hard to have a gift you can't talk to anyone about."

I was settling back down. He'd scared me coming up so quietly, though I knew when I was reading he didn't really need to be quiet. However, his familiarity with my gift made me uncomfortable. What else did he know that he might not be sharing?

"Win didn't do this," Morgan said. "I don't know how the intruder got in, but I expect those lights you saw were that person, trying to set her up."

"I was hoping that maybe I'd see who it was," I said.

"Miz Beverly never did learn how to do that," Morgan said. "She'd know things. If she knew the person well, she might figure who it was in her vision, or if she saw someone through another person's eyes she might know, but generally she just got impressions. She knew when I started how scared I was all the time, afraid she was going to turn me out if I did anything out of line. She put me at ease, always knew the right thing to say. It was years before I learned how she did it."

I smiled. "She liked you." I knew that, but I hadn't known how much Gram had trusted Morgan.

"Miz Beverly tended to like most folks. She didn't suffer fools, but she liked people."

I nodded.

"Your gift is why she left everything to you and not to Miz Marty," Morgan said.

"It is," I agreed.

"I wondered. What with Miz Marty here all the time and you were off on your own. Not that I didn't think she didn't love you or that you didn't deserve things, mind, but I wondered why you were so special to her. You see her Penelope Blue, too?"

"Did she tell you she saw her?"

"Miz Beverly saw most of her cats long after they'd passed," Morgan said. "And her horses. No people though. She said she couldn't."

"She never told me that." I was sort of upset that Gram had told Morgan more than me. Of course, I learned everything he talked about when I'd talked to her recently, but not before she'd died. Maybe she knew not to tell me. After all, I'd apparently talked to a much younger Gram, and she knew I didn't think I could talk to ghosts.

I followed him out of the new wing and into the main one. I heard the bell and Morgan hurried off to answer. I had no doubt it was Detective Cabot.

I heard them both in the entry and I went over there. Morgan ushered us into the formal living area, turning on lights. Cabot sat on the cream sofa. Morgan joined him. I took one of the pale green wingback chairs that were over by the window looking out, but I angled more towards them.

"Tell me about the lights you saw," Cabot asked me.

I told him what I saw from the carriage house

and how I'd gone over after they went out and found Morgan vacuuming.

"You were upstairs?" Cabot asked Morgan.

Morgan nodded.

He'd looked at home with the vacuum. Not only had he talked about not wanting to be upstairs, I knew he had arthritis in his knees. We'd talked about that before Gram died. I'd offered to help but he was reluctant to take me up on it. He wasn't even real keen on me hiring a part time person, even just for upstairs.

I didn't think he'd have had time to go up there and look as unflustered as he did running the vacuum, but perhaps I was wrong. It was odd that he'd just shown up beside me when I went to Win's room. Although, he could say the same about me.

If we wanted to distrust each other, I had the ability to have gone to Win's room and placed the syringe before going up to find Morgan. Maybe I was looking for a reason for my prints to be on the knob. I almost screamed out loud. I might have erased any fingerprints the police could have lifted, assuming that Officer Daffney hadn't already done so.

"You called the police in case someone was still in the house?" Cabot reiterated.

Morgan and I agreed.

"Daffney found no signs of forced entry or

anyone still in the house," Cabot said. "However, if both of you were upstairs with the vacuum, you wouldn't have heard someone leave, would you?"

I shook my head. I shuddered. I'd left the carriage house door unlocked. If someone had been in the big house planting the syringe, they could just as easily have been in my place.

Cabot's phone rang. He answered, listening carefully. His face hardened and he looked serious. He made a few noises of understanding before telling someone to text him the address.

"I have to go," he said standing up. "There's been an attack."

Chapter 36

Morgan and I looked at each other as we stood in the door looking after Detective Cabot. The mantel clock ticked behind us. I felt like it had meant a change in the world. I leaned back against the hardwood of the front door. Morgan just stood there, stunned.

"Who could it have been?" he wondered. I knew he was wondering who had been attacked.

I shook my head. If it had been someone in my family, surely Cabot would have told me, but once the thought crossed my mind, I couldn't get rid of it. I pulled out my phone, thankful that I tended to place it in pockets and carry it around with me. I called my mom.

She and my dad were home. In fact, it sounded as if I had woken her. I felt badly.

"I'm sorry," I said. "We thought we might have an intruder here, and then Detective Cabot had to leave because someone was attacked."

"An intruder?" My mom quickly came awake at the thought I might be in danger. "In the carriage house?"

"I saw lights in the big house," I said. "I came over here to talk to Morgan because Win was going to visit her mom. They were in her rooms. She came home when we called and told her, but I guess the officer here found a used syringe in her closet. He took her to the station for questioning. Cabot came over here to talk to us some more."

"Oh, dear lord." I heard my mom's voice shaking. She couldn't believe Win would do something like that, could she?

"The police walked through the house, and there's no one here that they could see. It's possible that with Morgan vacuuming upstairs that whoever was here could have slipped out then. They could even have stayed in the house after the wake."

"Your father and I are coming over. Have Morgan make up a room for us," my mom said. "And you'll stay there, in the room you used, not out at the carriage house. Either that or both of you are coming here. Morgan can use your brother's old room."

I looked at Morgan searching about for something to move or do in the big house. He wasn't going to feel comfortable at my folks' place. That would cross a line for him. I could try and get him to go to his kids, but I had a feeling he wouldn't go. Jaci lived over the barn, but while the two of them were friendly, they weren't buddies enough for Morgan to sleep on her sofa. Besides, he wasn't a young man any longer.

"It'd probably be easier to have you and dad come here. I'll tell Morgan."

"I'm calling Daisy, too. If this is related to what happened to Marty, better we're all together."

My mom would be the person saving the day in a horror movie. Everyone else would want to split up and search, and Mom would be like a herding dog rallying everyone together so no one got lost or hurt.

I hung up and looked at Morgan. "We have guests. And I've been ordered to sleep upstairs in my old room."

We knew my folks would be coming, so Morgan made up a room for them. We weren't sure about Daisy, but he made up a room for her anyway. I helped him change out the sheets that hadn't been used, though I suspected he and Win changed them out on a weekly basis, just to keep them fresh. I wondered about going back to the carriage house but decided I'd wait until my folks got there and I could take my dad with me.

While I wasn't exactly afraid, I worried about what my mom would say if she learned I'd gone off by myself.

Hellspark and Babs came out to investigate what we were doing. Penelope Blue didn't show herself to me. I was reminded that Morgan knew about Gram's talent and now he knew about mine. Had he been worried when he found me? Had he wondered what I knew? Could he have been the one to kill Marty?

Although my thoughts gave me a chill, I couldn't imagine him ever harming anyone, particularly not someone he loved like his own child.

As we walked down the stairs, looking around, watchful in ways we normally weren't, I asked Morgan, "Do you regret not being closer to your own family?"

He looked at me and shrugged. "My boy is a good boy. I was there when he was growing up, just in evenings and weekends, like most folks. It was only later, after he was grown and out of the house that my wife and I moved in here. It was kind of nice, like what they call that downsizing thing. Then when she was gone, Miz Beverly was getting on and she needed me more. It's not that I don't see my boy, but I don't have to live with him."

"I'm glad you're part of my family," I said, hugging him.

Morgan gave me a gentle hug back but then stepped into his role as worker. "I'll get some tea and put out some snacks, in case anyone's hungry. I have a feeling no one will be going right up to bed."

The house phone rang and Morgan answered it. He talked softly for a moment and then ended with, "Miz Ash gave me some names. I'll get right on it."

I looked up at him, frowning.

"That was Win. Her sister found her mother badly beaten a little bit ago. Her mom and sister are at the hospital. Her mom's unconscious. The police are questioning Win about it down at the station. She asked for her phone call to call a lawyer. Do you still have those names?"

Chapter 37

Morgan and I spent some time getting ahold of an attorney. Tara Tincher, one of the people Nick Spencer had recommended, had an answering service and either because she was the least busy or using Spencer's name had moved our names up on a legitimate list, she called us back about ten minutes after we'd reached the answering service.

She took some details from Morgan and promised to head down to the police station. My folks arrived at the house not long after that. Then I had to tell them everything. It was well after midnight when my dad walked me back to the carriage house to get a few things for that night.

"Do you think we're over-reacting?" I asked him.

"I would say no. I'm concerned about how many people have been hurt." His voice was quiet in the night. Around us frogs still croaked and crickets still sang, but not like they did earlier. A few late-night singers, I thought.

The air was clear and I didn't smell any rain in the breeze that came up every now and then. Just the faintest scent of the barn and the horses inside.

The next day came, but Win didn't return. Morgan called her to talk to see if she needed anything, but she wasn't answering her phone.

"How long can they keep her?" he asked.

None of us had an answer.

My dad left for work. My mom called Daisy. She hadn't wanted to leave her home in the middle of the night but wanted to be kept appraised of what was going on.

Daisy came by and sat with us, her turn to comfort the rest of us.

"It can't be Win," she said. "She had no reason to hurt Marty or Claire."

"Who would?" my mom asked. "I mean, yes, Claire Wilcox was a police officer, but Marty wasn't. So who would have a reason for both of them? And then Win's mom was badly beaten. I can't imagine Win doing that."

"Do you think I should go over there?" Daisy asked. "For solidarity?"

Of course we couldn't just go there because Win's mom's house was a crime scene. Her sister was probably at the hospital, but hospitals limited the number of visitors, so instead we did nothing.

The talk was depressing. I got up and paced around. I wondered who was trying to set Win up and why. It had to be a set up because otherwise why had there been a light on in her window. The fact that her mom was badly injured was another clue. The murderer wanted people to believe she'd hurt people even though anyone who met her knew she wasn't a violent person.

I know that people always say you never who could kill someone, but my gut was saying this was all wrong.

The police arrived with a warrant to do a further search on Win's rooms. Morgan called the attorney and her office said they could send an assistant, but Ms. Tincher was downtown with Win. Morgan let the police start searching Win's rooms.

I watched them from the hallway, as close as I could, feeling frustrated that I couldn't do anything. They went through all of Win's things carefully, not like people who cared about the owner but like those who were looking for something. I didn't know what. It made my stomach burn.

Detective Cabot wasn't there. I didn't know any of the officers who came, which surprised me. Living in a small town you start recognizing service people. As often as I'd had contact with the police, you'd have thought I'd recognize all of them.

Morgan joined me where I watched. We both wanted to make sure no one looked through anything that wasn't on the warrant. My understanding was that the warrant was limited to her living space and not the entire house. It wasn't that we had anything to hide, but it seemed only right to make sure they didn't look in places they weren't supposed to.

Ms. Tincher's assistant arrived when the search was about halfway through. She examined the warrant and took a photo of it to send her boss. Then she stood with us, making sure the police weren't doing anything they weren't supposed to.

I noticed that the police bagged up a number of items but couldn't exactly tell what they were. I hoped that there wasn't something else planted for them to find.

I finally went to the other room to sit with Mom and Daisy. We all huddled together and whispered things about the murders. Win's mom's attack made no sense. At least Marty and Claire were connected. Win's mom wasn't.

Unless the murderer was Win, but then why would someone be in her room when she wasn't there?

It was possible there was someone out there who suspected Win, but I just couldn't believe it. It didn't feel right.

But someone wanted the police to find that syringe on the floor. Win was neat and tidy. The weather was still hot, but it was cooling enough that she'd have looked in her closet. She wouldn't have left something like that on the floor for anyone to see. Someone had planted it, wanting to make it look like Win had killed Marty.

Worse, they'd even gone so far as to attack her mother. According to Tincher's assistant, a young man who looked just out of high school, if Win's sister hadn't come by when she did, Win's mom could easily have died from the beating. I wondered if whoever had done it was counting on that.

I shuddered to think there was someone who was willing to go to such lengths to get what they wanted.

Chapter 38

It was nearly dinner time when Detective Cabot arrived, bringing Win with him.

Mom hurried to her and gave her a hug. "Shouldn't you be at the hospital?" Mom asked.

Win didn't meet her eyes. "I can't right now. I needed to get a few things. I'll go when I've showered." She didn't glance at Cabot, who stayed silent, waiting.

Cabot and I looked at each other. He was easy on the eyes, even when he wasn't smiling. He looked concerned for all of us.

Once Win was out of earshot, my mom and Daisy hurrying with her, though what they were going to do for her once she was in the shower, I didn't know, he sighed.

He looked briefly at Morgan and my dad.

Then, his eyes returned to me.

"The syringe had no fingerprints on it. Wiped clean. That lends credence to your story about the light and the idea that the syringe was placed there by someone else. Win was on her way here when her mom was attacked. The timing for her to have hurt her mother before heading this way works, but barely," Cabot said.

"And you're telling us this why?" My dad drew himself up.

"Because I think there's something else going on and it seems to revolve around the people in this house, probably Ash. I think Win's mother was a distraction. It was pure luck that Win's sister, Lydia, came by when she did. That wasn't planned. Whoever is doing this is dangerous, and you all need to be warned. I'm having officers watching the place." Cabot looked at all three of us again, leaving his eyes on me the longest.

"Maybe we should hire someone?" Morgan suggested. "I can find out the names of good security from the attorneys, I'm sure."

"I'd say that's a good idea. It might be linked to Mrs. Beauvoir's death, but it might be something else. However, I don't like the fact that everything links back to this house or to someone in it."

Faintly, I heard water start. Mom and Daisy hurried out of the new wing.

"That poor girl," Daisy said. "You didn't honestly believe that she'd beat her own mother?" She addressed that last part to Cabot.

"We have to investigate all possibilities, ma'am," Cabot said. "However, the bruising was consistent with someone stronger and taller than Win. Plus, her neighbors saw her mother moving around in the kitchen, or a woman who looked like her, after Win had left. It's not impossible she doubled back. Because witnesses' memories of time can be fudged, it's still just barely within the realm of possibility. I needed to question her thoroughly in case she knew something that might help us."

"Did she know that's why you were questioning her?" Mom demanded.

Cabot smiled. "I don't go around suggesting to people that I'm not going arrest them until I'm sure I won't. There are too many questions for me to have done that for Win. Since the evidence against her is sketchy at best, I feel safe enough saying something now, but I'd advise her to keep her attorney in case that changes."

So Cabot had the same questions and thoughts I did. All of it revolved around this place. It started with Marty. Claire wouldn't have gotten close to the killer because she was focused on me, so she wasn't targeted because she got to close to the killer. Win's mom was likely a target to make the police look at Win.

I sighed. I wasn't cut out to be a detective. I just couldn't fathom what would make someone kill another person.

Cabot talked to us a little more, asking us what we knew about Gram's will. Certainly he could have asked anyone at Erickson, Carter, and Moss. He probably had, but what was actually in the will and what we thought we understood about what was in it might be subtly different.

"And your brother?" Cabot asked, looking at me.

"He stayed in a hotel last night. He headed back to Charlotte today," I said.

"You didn't have him stay here?"

"He could have," Morgan said, "but he didn't call and ask. He thought no one was allowed to use the place until Marty's challenge to the will was done with. We'd have put him up easily. I made sure to let him know, that."

"That's what he told me, too," I said.

Cabot was making notes as if this was all new, but I couldn't help but think he'd been over this time and again. Why wasn't there any evidence?

"I just wish we had some idea of who would do this." I was thinking out loud, voicing what I knew everyone else wanted to know.

"It appeared to start when Marty challenged the will," Cabot said. We'd gone over that before.

I nodded.

"What else changed then?" Cabot pressed. "Anything?"

"We got a new organist at the church around that time," Daisy tossed out. "Marty hadn't met her but it was right then. I can't imagine she had anything to do with it."

"She have any family around here or was she new in town?" Cabot asked.

"She lives down in Lawrenceburg. It's a bit of a drive but there aren't many Lutheran churches around here," Daisy said. "I can't imagine how that changed anything, but it was something new. She played for the first time the Sunday before Marty…"

Cabot got the woman's name just in case but he didn't seem to think that was related.

I tried to think back to what else was going on just before Marty challenged the will.

"Everything was sort of up in the air," my mom said. "Mom had just died and there was the funeral and the will. We had people from out of town. The wake happened here, of course. Half the town came. People we hadn't seen in years."

I nodded. If Marty's wake had been big, Gram's had been huge. We'd had more food and more people and it had gone on long into the night with plenty of memories shared.

"Anyone who might have stuck around?" Cabot asked.

"Lots of people live around here, but we just don't see them often," my mom said. "I can't think of anyone I've suddenly had much contact with that had I hadn't had before."

I shook my head. "I feel like I should be a suspect again. I'm the one person who only got here a few months ago." I probably shouldn't have said it like that, but it came out.

"Which may mean this is about you," Cabot said. "Anyone you know who would want to hurt you?"

I shrugged. "Not that I know of. I guess if someone were hiding it from me, maybe my friend Cheri would know more. Or Eric." I didn't think Thad would have listened to much gossip, so he was likely out.

Cabot made notes. "I'll look both of them up. For now, I think it's best that you stay with your family here. If you go anywhere, make sure someone else is around."

We all nodded and watched him leave.

Win came out when he was gone. She'd been crying but she looked fresher than when she'd come in.

"Let me take you to the hospital," Mom said.

Win tried to wave her off, but Mom was firm. "You can call me to pick you up or your sister probably has a car. She can bring you back if you don't want to call, but after a day like today, you shouldn't be driving that far. I'd be a mess if it were me."

"You shouldn't be alone," my dad said. "So I'll drive both of you. We can pick up something for dinner on the way, unless you're not hungry, in which case, we'll do it on the way back."

Mom and Win looked at each other but let him take the lead.

That left me and Daisy and Morgan.

"We should order in," Morgan said. "It'll be festive."

I let him get on the phone to call someone to deliver food. What I really wanted was a hot bath, but that would probably have to wait. I just couldn't stop the feeling that I was waiting for the other shoe to drop and something bad was going to happen.

Chapter 39

Three days passed and nothing happened. I lived in the big house and was getting antsy to go back to my little carriage house. My folks decided to head back to their house, with the agreement that when they would wait at Gram's—well, my place—until both were ready to go home. That way neither would be alone.

Daisy stayed at the house with me, Morgan, and Win. I talked to her about whether she might like to live there and take it over. We talked about her dream of a bed and breakfast.

"I just couldn't do it," she said. "Not here. Too many memories. I always thought that it would be something to leave Marty, but I don't have that now. Who would want to run a B&B once I was gone?"

I let her talk. I certainly had no interest in running a bed and breakfast, so we let that idea go. However, she did seem interested in living in the big house.

"Are you sure?" she asked me three or four times each day after I mentioned it.

I was. I was pleased that she wanted to be there. That meant I wouldn't be so alone out in the carriage house. Alone had never bothered me before, but I had never really thought about how much mental space Gram had taken up. Someone needed to be in the big house besides Morgan and Win. I was glad it was going to be my aunt.

"If Marty had known," Daisy said one day, "I wonder if she would have challenged the will. Of course, if Claire was the one pushing for her to do so, and I think she was, then maybe it wouldn't have mattered to her at all."

"Why would Clairc bc so interested?" I asked. We were sitting in the great room, having tea, looking out across the lawn. The tulip poplars in the fields behind the hedge of viburnum and laurel waved slightly in the breeze outside.

Hellspark was curled on Daisy's lap, a single paw hanging off her legs. Babs was on the back of the sofa, halfway between us. While she might have been keeping her distance from both of us, I couldn't help but think she was keeping a more wary eye on me. Did even the cats think I was a murderer?

"I think she really thought she was trying to help straighten Marty up, but she just made her selfish, or more selfish," Daisy said. "Marty didn't always speak up when she needed to, you know. She'd just whine about things after. She worked hard at her job and tried to be good, but when someone criticized her, she didn't know how to handle it. She'd talk it out later, but she wouldn't do anything. She probably mentioned not getting much in the will. Claire may have decided this was the time Marty should stand up for herself. I think something like that happened with Landon."

"What do you mean?"

"Marty let Landon make a lot of decisions about what was happening in their relationship. I think Claire wanted her to be more assertive. Marty's not good at that, so she started complaining to Landon about everything she didn't like, whether it was the shirt he was wearing, or the fact that he got stuck in traffic on the way home from work and was ten minutes late to meet her, even though he called." Daisy shook her head. "I think he finally got tired of it. From what he said, it sounds like she was doing that to a lot of people. It would have passed, you know. Marty was a drama queen, but she wasn't normally mean about it."

I nodded. Daisy was right. Marty might go off and complain and whine, but she didn't need to be mean. I had seen a little bit of her new-found assertiveness when I'd come home. She'd been very clear that she wanted some alone time with Gram. I had put it down to losing our grandmother and let her have the times she wanted. Marty was still working but I wasn't.

"It's too bad she didn't assert herself by talking to me," I said. "Instead, she just got an attorney and made everyone miserable."

Daisy nodded. "That was typical of Marty though. She'd have hated talking, you know. It was far easier to let someone else do the talking, even if that someone else was an attorney. I keep thinking that whatever got her and Claire killed, it was about the will."

"But you know I didn't kill her," I said.

Daisy nodded. "I know. I wonder if maybe it was somcone who thought they were protecting you? Maybe it was someone who was angry at her for challenging the will."

I frowned. I couldn't think of who that would be.

"Then why Officer Wilcox?" I asked. I couldn't call her Claire like my aunt. She was a police officer.

Daisy shook her head. "That I don't know. Nor do I know why they'd go after Win's mother, not now that the police seem to think you weren't involved."

"Unless they didn't really know," I said, thinking about it.

Later, I called Cheri and talked with her. There were still rumors floating around that I was under suspicion for Marty's death.

"That LeAnn just won't let go. I don't know why she's so hot about it, although you did say Landon was her cousin, but I haven't heard anything that suggests they were at all close."

"Maybe the fear of having a murderer in the family?" I asked.

Cheri snorted but we continued tossing around ideas.

"Anything about why someone would kill Officer Wilcox?"

"Generally people think it's related to your cousin's death," Cheri said. "I've heard that she and Marty knew something, that you killed both of them, that your dad killed them both, that Landon was mad because he wanted people to know that he'd killed Marty, although why he wouldn't just confess made no sense, but you know how people are."

"And Win?"

"Some folks are saying she just snapped under all that stress. A few people think it's drug related. Others are wondering if maybe Win heard something between Marty and Landon or maybe about you at the big house, and this was a warning to keep her mouth shut."

So now I wasn't just a murderer, I was a crime lord. Well, that was interesting.

"Anything else?"

Cheri didn't have much else on Win's mom's injury. We talked about how scary this was. It wasn't like Seales had a ton of murders and these all seemed to be related. Here I was at the center. I didn't mention Daisy's idea that there was someone out there thinking they were protecting me.

It was almost like that felt too true to speak out loud. I didn't want to give voice to it, in case it made it real. I didn't want to think I was someone others thought they might have to protect. Not by killing people, at least.

Chapter 40

By the end of the fourth day, I was pretty stir crazy. I had finally gotten my acupuncture license, so I made plans to start calling around about clinic space. My life had been on hold long enough. I had dinner in the big house with Morgan, Win, and Daisy. Daisy was making plans to have her things moved into the room she was using in the big house. She wasn't using Gram's room, of course, but one just across the hallway.

Win was taking a break from the hospital. Her mother was doing better, if an unconscious person could be said to do so. Her vitals were stronger, and the nurses said there was more brain activity. Doctors were hopeful that she might wake up soon. Despite that, everyone needed a break now and then. Win had come back to shower and change. Looking at the time, she decided it would be good to make some chicken for dinner.

We talked of everything but the murders. By the time Win and Morgan started cleaning up, I was ready to head back to the carriage house and plan my day.

Once in the carriage house, it was too quiet. Maybe I needed to reconsider living in the big house. At least there were people around. I remembered wanting to take Hellspark and Babs, though I remembered how he had cuddled on Daisy's lap last evening.

I turned on the radio and started working on the computer. I always left the blinds up in the little breakfast room, even at night, but that night, I kept thinking someone was looking at me.

I got up and pulled them.

Penelope Blue appeared on my desk, prancing around like cats do when you're trying to work.

"What is it?" I askcd hcr.

She opened her mouth like she was meowing, but all I heard was a tiny, echoing squeak.

I heard something that sounded like a scream.

I headed to the door to look out.

The night was just dark enough to confuse me. There was motion and movement, but I couldn't make it out for an instant.

Finally, I realized I was watching two people struggling. I thought one was Win. She'd probably been walking to her car. Someone was tugging at her head, pulling her down and backwards at an angle that had to hurt.

I reached back for my phone, tripping on the step. The music I'd been listening to floated out into the night air. Win's attacker looked up.

He was taller than Win. Taller than me. He was dressed all in black, including a ski mask, which is not something commonly seen in Kentucky. Certainly not in late summer.

He hit Win over the head again, dropping her body while I tried to find my phone. I was searching around on the table near the door, not wanting to take my eyes off the man.

He walked towards me, each foot moving slowly.

I screamed, hoping Morgan or Daisy would hear. Or even Jaci.

The gravel crunched under his boots.

He moved in a way that seemed familiar.

I tried to place it.

I stepped backwards, feeling for the phone.

I reached it, the cool feel of the case against my hand a saving grace.

I pushed against the front door to slam it closed just as he reached it.

We struggled with the door.

I threw my entire body against it.

I heard it latch. I turned the lock and backed

up into my tiny kitchen. As if that would save me if he broke down the door.

The intruder banged on the door again.

Penelope Blue appeared in front of me and then faded out. I turned towards her as she pranced in front of the bay windows before disappearing again. I turned around, wondering what she was doing.

Behind me, glass shattered.

He'd been out there.

I punched in 911, but the intruder was through the window, knocking the phone away before I could say a word.

The force of the blow sent a cold shiver of pain up my arm.

I groaned.

I am not a fighter. I am not a large person.

I looked around for something to fight with. I backed towards the kitchen island, with the goal of finding a knifc.

"Don't." The voice belonged to Rick Darlingon. He was reaching out a hand towards me.

Pieces fell into place. I knew the way he walked. He'd never wanted the break up, but I'd had to go. He'd resented that.

"You?" I hissed, frozen for a moment.

"I couldn't let you leave. Not again," he said.

So it wasn't about protecting me so much as keeping me there.

"But…" I started.

"That damned cop was sure you did it. I figured without her around, they'd stop looking at you. She just wouldn't let it go. I saw them even if you didn't," Rick said. "I needed them to focus on someone else."

"Win did nothing to you." I didn't yell. I didn't hiss. I just said it. I had found in my clinic sometimes that's the best way to get an idea across. Don't make an issue of it.

"Win didn't defend you!" Rick snapped.

I wondered if the 911 operator was hearing this. I wondered if Morgan had heard me scream. Was he also calling the police?

"I didn't need defending," I snapped. Now I was getting mad.

Rick pulled the ski mask off and was walking towards me. "Now that you're staying, we can get back together."

"We are not going to get back together," I said. "That's just not happening."

"We're better together. You wouldn't have solved your problems without me."

Rick had always been something of a bulldozer, though I'd not known him to be physical.

"You dated Marty," I said.

"She wasn't you."

I was now around the island. Penelope Blue was at the front door, prancing beside it.

"And Cheri." Although shouldn't Cheri have figured out how obsessed he was? Or hadn't she said he wasn't over me yet? I couldn't remember. Now wasn't the time to try.

"I'm sorry," Rick said. "I thought maybe she'd tell you and you'd want to come back. I couldn't believe it when you did."

"It wasn't for you." Was he that much of a narcissist? "It was because Gram was dying."

"But you were back." Rick was pleading now. I was near the table where my computer was. He was behind the island. I hadn't gotten a knife.

My feet crunched on broken glass. I was wearing slippers with rubber soles, so at least I wasn't going to get my feet cut up.

Jagged edges of glass lined the window. I could slip out of there if I wanted to chance the cuts. I wasn't sure Rick would let me through. If he tackled me as I tried to climb through the window, I could hit something vital and bleed out before help arrived. If I was going to die, I was going to die fighting.

I moved away from the window, leading Rick back towards the main room.

I scanned the place but the fireplace had no poker. I had a few books, a lamp. I could use the lamp if I had to, but it wasn't exactly a club. The front door was locked and it would take me a minute to unlock it. I'd probably have to turn my back to him. Even if I backed up towards it, Rick would hurry to catch me.

He hadn't thought through what would happen next. Maybe he just wanted to hurt Win or perhaps she'd seen him stalking me. I'd felt like someone was watching that evening.

"Why did you try and hurt Win?" I asked.

"She saw me and screamed," Rick said. "I had to shut her up. I wanted to surprise you."

"I'm still surprised," I said.

Rick smiled a little. Was he that bad off? He wasn't making sense.

"We have to go away. I'm sorry. I wanted you stay, but if I can't stay anymore, you need to come with me," Rick said. He seemed more sorry that we had to leave than that he'd killed my cousin.

"You killed my family," I growled.

"Just Marty."

Like Marty didn't matter at all.

I screamed at him, rushing towards him, surprising him. I hit him in the face, going for his nose. I missed, and he grabbed my arm.

I brought my knee up to his groin.

He jumped back.

My foot slammed down as hard as I could on his instep.

His grip loosened.

Arm free, I ducked and slammed my arm into

his kneecap, driving it backwards at an angle knees weren't supposed to go.

Rick gasped and fell back.

I ran for the door, unlocking it.

I had hardly turned, but was planning to run for the big house, when someone else grabbed me.

Chapter 41

I screamed, suddenly certain that Rick wasn't working alone.

"It's okay," a familiar voice said. "It's me. Police."

Detective Cabot. He was pulling me away from the carriage house as Officer Daffney went in, gun drawn. I shuddered.

"Stay where you are," Daffney said, clearly directing his words to Rick. Another officer followed and cuffed him.

When that was done, I breathed out a sigh.

"Did my 911 call go through?" I asked.

Cabot nodded. "We still had people driving by regularly. Daffney heard a scream even before you called. He called in an attack. He was going to help Win when your attacker went for the door. I was already on my way."

I nodded. I wanted to ask why they'd waited so long to come in but probably it hadn't been as long as it had felt in the room. Besides, Daffney was alone and Win was hurt. Flashing red lights from a medic unit appeared. They were there to help her.

"I can't believe he did this," I said. "I mean, Rick. He was always harmless."

"People change," Cabot said. He led me to the big house to sit me down and warm up.

"You can't stay out there until we get it cleaned up," Morgan said.

"It's a crime scene," Cabot added.

I nodded. Daisy slipped out of the room, probably to call my mom. Morgan made tea.

I told Cabot what had happened. He asked questions about Rick's motivations. I explained what he'd said.

"You always said you'd stay around anyway, so he never needed to do that," Cabot said.

"He also didn't need to try and kill Win's mother. He was listening to what the gossip said. He didn't know I wouldn't leave. Someone probably thought I would. He also didn't seem to know that I wasn't the main focus of the murder investigation any longer, probably thanks to LeAnn VanderPlank."

Cabot nodded and finished making more notes. I sipped hot tea. Daisy came and sat with me, listening, patting my arm.

"I recommend going to the hospital and being checked over," Cabot said.

"I'll be fine. Is it possible for me to get my things from the carriage house?"

We discussed the logistics of that. I wasn't allowed to go in but I could make a list of things I wanted and one of the officers would pack a bag. I would not be getting my phone. Rick had fallen on top of it when he went down. It was now considered evidence.

A trip to the phone store was in my future.

"We'll take care of her here," Morgan assured him. Daisy added her voice. If that wasn't enough, my mom walked in about that time and started managing everyone.

Cabot gave me a long smile and nodded. I waved at him.

"He's a nice looking man," my mom said. "Do you suppose he's married?"

"I didn't see a ring," Daisy pointed out, giving me her own smile. I had to wonder if Uncle Ted hadn't married her because she had her own level of psychic ability. It was completely different from mine, but he'd have been used to that with Gram.

Chapter 42

A week later I was starting to get comfortable in the big house. Before it had always been Gram's. It was finally starting to sink in that it was mine.

Still, I liked having my own space. I wanted more than just a room in the large house. I wanted a place to wander into the kitchen where I could fix myself a snack, a place to hang out and do nothing without anyone asking if I needed something. So, when the police released the carriage house, I immediately moved back in. If I hated doing my own laundry, I could probably take it over to the big house.

Win was already back at work, though Morgan and Daisy were insisting she take it easy. I added my voice to that, but no one seemed to listen to me. Everyone wanted to cater to me as if I were the one who had been wounded.

Win's mom woke up the day after Win went to the hospital for her own injuries. She was horrified by what had happened to her daughter. Rick hadn't worn a ski mask when he beat her up, probably expecting that she'd have died. We were lucky she didn't. Her testimony added to mine was likely to keep Rick in jail for a good long time.

After helping Morgan clean up around the kitchen—we had ordered a new window right after the breakage and put a rush on it—when the glass was gone and it was just the usual construction mess, I called Cheri. She met me for a late afternoon tea and gossip.

"I can't believe that it was Rick," Cheri said. "I knew he was kind of obsessed with you, but I had no idea…"

I nodded. "I kept thinking that it was Landon or someone who hated him."

"You just never know. I mean I know your Gram tended to know things, but now that she's gone, where will we turn?"

I must have looked startled.

"Oh, don't think that the entire town doesn't know that Mrs. Beauvoir knew things. No one ever knew how, but she did. If she said that someone was acting strangely, we all watched. If she had a favorite horse, we all paid attention to that horse," Cheri prattled on.

"I guess I took Gram's abilities for granted," I said slowly.

Cheri nodded. "I always thought you didn't want to live in the house because you knew she saw ghosts there or something."

I laughed a little. "No." I wondered about sharing with Cheri that I had my own talents. I thought about it, sipping my tea, a lovely orange spice that I'd found in a little hole-in-the-wall shop in Frankfort.

Cheri chattered on about other things people knew and the moment passed. Penelope Blue settled on the sofa next to me, looking at Cheri and then at me. I breathed out thinking that perhaps I could tell people about my gifts and people would tolerate them far better than I believed. Daisy knew about Gram and was fine. She even guessed a bit about me.

Morgan knew both about me and Gram and didn't mind. He'd been perfectly fine when I'd gone around touching things to see what I could learn in Win's apartment.

Apparently most of the town had known about Gram. It seemed that my mother was the only one who had issues with psychics. Still, I wasn't going to blurt out to Cheri about my own gifts. I might be learning that it was okay to know things simply by touching them, and maybe even to see ghosts, but I wasn't quite ready to open up that much, not even to my best friend. Kentucky is a rather conservative place when it comes to things like that.

I got a text while we were talking. I glanced at it and I must have raised my eyebrows.

"What is it?" Cheri asked.

"Detective Cabot wants to know if there's a good time to call me," I said.

"I thought the case was all done?"

"I did, too."

Cheri looked at me and told me to tell him any time.

I did so. The phone rang moments later.

After a few rather awkward greetings and a comment that yes, the case was over, Cabot asked if I wanted to have coffee sometime.

I agreed.

Cheri's eyes were big and her smile about broke her face in half when I hung up.

"I knew it! I knew he was interested in you! And you said yes!" She bounced up and down hard enough that Penelope Blue disappeared. In fact, she didn't just fade as she usually did, she popped out.

"I think you're more excited than I am," I said.

"I love a good romance!" Cheri announced and made squee noises again.

While I was looking forward to getting to know Detective Byron Cabot a bit better, I had to admit I wasn't sure if I was ready for Cheri's excitement. Still, now that my acupuncture license had come through, and I'd seen one really good space that I hoped to rent, Kentucky was looking up. An admirer—a sane admirer, I corrected—would be just the thing to keep life interesting.

Author's Note

Anyone who drives through Central Kentucky from Versailles to Frankfort will know I played fast and loose with geography in that area. There is no Seales and no Bram County. However, the town itself was inspired by Woodford County, Kentucky, and its environs, which residents will recognize.

All of the people are purely fictional. I have taken great liberties with the small police department in Seales and made it fit what I needed.

Ash's friends from Vancouver, Washington—Lisa and Barb—are inspired by friends from acupuncture school and acupuncture practice. Neither of them have had to keep a secret about my psychic abilities because I have none. Like Ash, I miss my friends (not just Lisa and Barb) from the

Pacific Northwest, but this part of my life has taken me elsewhere and made me learn that there are many places in the U.S. that are beautiful and have their own flavor.

Enjoy your reading, and if you get a chance to drive through Kentucky, enjoy the ride through some beautiful rolling hills.

About Bonnie Elizabeth

Bonnie Elizabeth could never decide what to do, so she wrote stories about amazing things and sometimes she even finished them.

While rejection stung her so badly in person, she spent most of her young life talking to cats and dogs rather than people, she was unusually resilient when it came to rejections on her writing, racking up a good number of them.

Floating through a variety of jobs, including veterinary receptionist, cemetery administrator, and finally acupuncturist, she continued to write stories.

When the internet came along (yes she's old), she started blogging as her cat, because we all know cats don't notice rejection. Then she started publishing.

Bonnie writes in a variety of genres. Her popular Whisper series is contemporary fantasy and her Teenage Fairy Godmother series is written for teens. She has been published in a number of anthologies and is working on expanding her writing repertoire.

She lives with her husband (who talks less than she does) and her three cats, who always talk back.

Stay in Touch

Also by Bonnie Elizabeth

The Whisper Novels

Whisper Bound

Taken by the Sound

An Air of Suspicion

Little Dog Lost

Death Interrupted

Down in Whisper

A Haunting Whisper

A Haunting Attraction

Secrets Not Whispers

Only Human

Appalachian Souls Series

Souls Lost

Souls Broken

Other Novels

One Bad Wish

Sun Spot Magic

Ghosts from the Past

Unnatural Secrets

Find them all at your favorite bookseller or check us out at MyBigFatOrangeCat.com